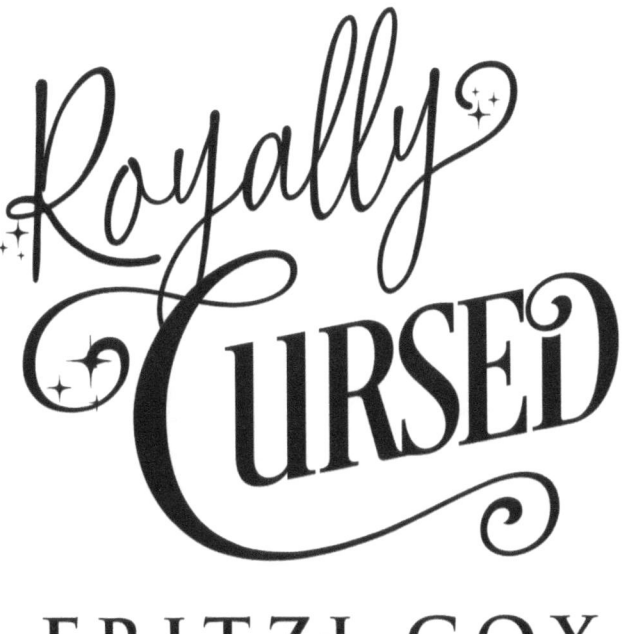

FRITZI COX

I0610393

Visit my website at, www.fritzicox.com
Cover Designer: Najla Qamber, www.najlaqamberdesigns.com
Editor: Jovana Shirley, Unforeseen Editing, www.unforeseenediting.com

ISBN-13: 978-1-7364167-2-3

CONTENTS

FROM THE DESK OF FRITZI COX

Confession: My name isn't Fritzi Cox. Due to the nature of my work, I write under an alias.

I'm a full-time reporter turned novelist and married to a reformed genie who no longer resides in the mystical realm. I saved him from a vicious curse to live for eternity in his big blue dildo. I couldn't make this up if I tried. I'm telling you my story, so you understand the events that transpire in this book.

If you'd like full details of my adventure, you can read Kat Addams's, *Ghosted.* But fair warning: I've changed our names to further protect our identities during this deadly crisis. After Penelope called me from jail and told me about the massacre, I knew I was no longer safe.

I also want this recount of events to serve as a historical document for myself in case something goes wrong in my coming days. I'm privy to top-secret information, and it's without question that I believe I'll soon be able to report from the other side. But I have a family to protect and a duty to report these stories as truthfully as I can. The following novel is based on the information given to me directly from the characters themselves. Anything I wrote, I had to get permission from the victims to report. There are still things I've left unsaid for their protection, my and my family's protection, and yours.

Please be advised: As with life, things aren't always rosy, and if you're reading this, tread cautiously. I'm afraid you've already learned too much.

CHAPTER ONE

PENELOPE

I CURLED MY FINGERS AROUND THE FRIGID IRON BARS AND
stuck my face through the gap before shouting to the guard
down the hall, "Please, sir! I promise I'm not violent or
mischievous." I paused, realizing the last trait was a lie. But I
quickly recovered. "Or up to no good. Just let me out. Please
let me wait for my friend out there."

I glanced behind me at the older woman bent over and
snoring atop a grimy metal toilet. She wore a tattered plaid
jacket and jogging pants pushed down around her ankles.
Her face sagged with deep wrinkles etched across her forehead like a map, drawing her problems out for all to see. The
folds of her jaw hung loosely around her mouth, molding her
expression into a permanent frown. I could smell the strong
scent of whiskey on her from across the room.

"I'll be on my best behavior!" I pleaded, scrunching my
nose and gripping the cell door even harder, as if I could
bend the bars further apart and slip out in between them.

"Sir?" I asked again.

No response.

I pressed my face between the metal bars one last time and took a deep breath before returning to the thin mattress against the wall. I carefully hopped between tiles caked with mildew, stale urine, and what looked like old blood until I found a somewhat-clean spot to rest my heels, which were also covered in blood—my ex-fiancé's blood.

My eyes squeezed shut as I tried to push away the horror I'd felt when I saw his fat head come clean off his neck and roll to my feet, a look of shock still lingering in his eyes. I rubbed my chest, aware of every rapid pulse my heart made these days, and wondered if Vail could still feel my heartbeat from where he was.

The helpless look on his face when I'd faded in his arms was forever seared into my memory. I couldn't save my friends, my godmother, and most certainly myself. But I knew Vail. Once the sun tucked beneath the horizon, he would begin to track me down in a heartbeat—my heartbeat. I just wasn't sure I wanted to be found. Wherever I went, death followed. He was better off without me.

I scooted myself across the scratchy cot and rested my back against the pitted concrete wall. A blast of cold air shot down from a vent above me, but I refused to touch the pilled, stained blanket curled at the top of the bed. I would rather snuggle with a troll than cover myself in something like a mummy wrapping, complete with the scent of the dead.

My eyes flew open at the sound of footsteps echoing down the hall. I held my breath and remained still, silently praying I wasn't getting another inmate. The young guard appeared around the corner, slowly shuffling his feet to the cell's latch while jingling a set of keys in his palm.

"Looks like today is your lucky day. You get a get-out-of-jail-free card," he said with a twang in his voice. He pressed a key into the lock and turned it until the lock clicked and the cell opened.

"I beg your pardon. What's that? Like a birthday card?" I hopped to my heels, scurrying across the dirty floor and out of my cage before he changed his mind.

"Ha!" He laughed. "Your friend told me you were ... mental. I already knew you weren't drunk. Just crazy."

"I'm not crazy!" My nostrils flared.

A heat rose inside me, urging to bubble out into a hellacious curse. But I couldn't perform magic anymore—or at least any spells that I knew.

I'd tried when the officer stopped me as I walked down the side of an abandoned road. I pointed at him with my hands, spreading my fingers wide, and chanted a spell I hoped would expose the wolfish tail he hid under his pants. I had every intention of questioning him and his whereabouts during the Bostwick Massacre.

But my spell didn't work. The officer only rubbed the back of his neck and took a step away from me. So, I took matters into my own hands and demanded he take his pants off and show me his tail at once. I'd had enough of his nonsense. The werewolves worked with the vampires, and I was also a part of that tribe. If this dog didn't cooperate, he would have to answer to my vampire boyfriend.

But as my luck would have it, it turned out that I was no longer in Morningwood, and the officer wasn't a werewolf. After I tried to slip behind him and peek under his trousers myself, he twisted my wrists around my back and locked them in metal rings in no time. That was the moment I realized I was dealing with a human. I had been so disoriented and in shock from the deadly night that I didn't know I'd left the magical realm.

And after hours spent in this horrible place, there was no hint of my return back home.

"Sure, you're not crazy. You just sexually harassed an officer. Look, I get it, lady. Women love men in uniform. But I think you drank more red wine than you spilled there on those pretty little shoes of yours. You can't go around, demanding we take our pants off. Although I'm sure some officers would have for a pretty thing like you." He licked his lips, openly skimming my figure.

When I didn't answer, he tilted his head and motioned for me to follow him down the hall. He pushed a button on the door and buzzed us through to the other side. Fritzi stood up from a chair in the waiting area and rushed to me.

"Fresh out of the drunk tank." The officer leaned against the door, watching my reunion with the only human I knew.

"Drunk tank? She doesn't look drunk to me! Did you give her a breathalyzer? What laws did she break?"

"Of course we did. It was low, but—"

"But?" Fritzi's eyes snapped to the officer.

"But she assaulted an officer and tugged at his pants. You know, like tried to get at his junk." He chewed his bottom lip, exposing a row of crooked teeth.

"You can clearly see my friend is mentally deranged. And you locked her up! You imprisoned a person with a mental health condition! I don't see her drinking either. She's not mentally stable enough! Someone slipped her something. This is a much bigger story." She stared back at me. "And why is your dress hanging off you like that, Penelope? Did someone touch you?" She rummaged through her purse, pulling out a pen and a small spiral notebook full of notes and scribbles. "Officer, what's your name?"

The officer backed away, holding his hands in the air. "Whoa, whoa, whoa. There's nothing to see here. Look, she gets a get-out-of-jail-free card. No harm, no foul. We had to put her in there. I didn't know what else to do with her. There's no one here to help with mental health. Blame the city and budget cuts. But she's free to go."

Fritzi eyed the officer before stuffing her writing materials back into her purse. I rubbed my wrists and looked toward the exit. A camera sat, tucked away in the corner of the ceiling, recording our exchange.

"Good day, Officer. I'm going to get my friend home. I'm sure you'll agree she's unwell, and she needs to be treated with care at once—the right kind of care. Goodness knows, she doesn't need any more abuse." Fritzi draped her arm over my shoulders and led me out the door.

I squinted, shielding my eyes from the sun's intense rays.

"I'm—" I started, following behind her.

"Shh. Not yet." She shook her head, hurrying across the parking lot.

A plastic cup fell from a full trash bin and rolled across our path. Fritzi kicked it out of the way and continued until we reached her car.

"This is us. Get in," she ordered me, nodding at the passenger side. "And buckle up. We've got about a forty-minute drive to the city."

I made my way around the car and slipped inside, ruffling my dress. It smelled like old food and paper. Behind me, a tiny seat sat empty. The pink material was covered in stains and fraying at the bottom.

"Do you transport gnomes?" I asked, strapping myself in the way the sheriff werewolf, Antonio, had taught me not long ago.

"Gnomes?" Fritzi laughed, following my gaze toward the gadget in the back. "That's not for gnomes! That's for my daughter."

"Oh. You're a mom?" I eyed her suspiciously.

She didn't look like a mother. Her eyes weren't tired, her skin had a youthful glow, and she looked—for lack of better words—put together. I hadn't crossed many mothers in my life, but I knew moms of small children usually exhibited every bit of exhaustion from their family. It played across their eyes in crow's-feet and across their stomachs from good intentions of not wasting uneaten cookies left on their child's plate. So, Fritzi must be a witch.

She started the engine and pulled away. "Yes, I'm a mom. And a wife. And a reporter. And—"

"A witch!" I pushed myself against the car door, creating more space between us.

"Definitely not that."

"Prove it."

"Well, for one, the handful of times we've met, I've told you I want to get back to the magic world. If I were a witch, I would be there. For two, if I were a witch, I'd be rich and have everything I wanted, including a nanny and house-keeper. Instead, I have a husband. And for three—" She swerved the car onto a busy street lined with brick buildings and evergreen shrubs.

"Okay, okay." I waved my hand in the air, stopping her. "I'm just shaken. I don't know who to trust anymore."

"I understand. For what it's worth, you can trust me. I know you don't know me well. Hey, how did you find me anyway?" she asked.

"I told them I needed to speak to Fritzi Cox. They got really quiet and let me make the call."

A smirk played across her lips. "Good. They know who I am. That's why the officer left you alone. The police depart-ment has had a lot of drama in the last year. They don't want any more. And me? I tell all. I shout it to the public from the rooftops. I've made a name for myself." She drummed her fingers on her steering wheel and smiled.

"Well, thanks for saving me. Where am I anyway?"

"Outer Forks."

"Hmm. I've never heard of Outer Forks, let alone been here. Anytime I fade, I don't end up far. I'm not sure why this time was different. I thought I was in Morningwood still until that officer threw me in the back of his car." I rested my head against the cool glass window and watched the other cars pass.

"Think you'll disappear again?" She glanced at me out of the corner of her eye before focusing back on the road.

"No."

"Why?"

"Because I lost everything I had back there. I have no reason to go back," I said.

"What about Vail? The cause?"

"I'm only trouble. If it wasn't for me, everyone would still be alive, and none of this would have happened. I should stay away. And as for the cause, everything was destroyed. It'll take a long time to get the equipment and data or whatever the hell they need up and running again."

"Sounds to me like you're making excuses."

"I am."

"You don't want to go back?"

"No."

We rode in silence until she turned off the busy road and stopped at a railroad crossing. The train barreled in front of us, blaring its horn, causing me to wince.

Fritzi turned in her seat and stared in my direction. "I know you already told me some of what happened when you called from jail. But I need the entire truth if I'm going to help you in whatever it is you choose to do. You're living in an entirely different world now. That will require a lot of work on your part—and mine. You have to tell me about last night. And it's going to be hard for you, I know. But I need all the details. We can figure it out from there. Together, okay? You aren't alone."

She reached out and patted my hand, the same way my godmother used to when she grew concerned. Her gesture alone soothed my soul and wrapped me in a tight comfort I couldn't explain. A touch like that was impossible to learn. It only came naturally to a mother.

"Why are you being so nice to me?" I looked away, hiding my wet eyes.

The train clacked down the tracks in a lulling rhythm, making me drowsy and suddenly aware of my exhaustion.

"Because I know what it's like to lose someone." She raised her voice above another whistle from the train.

"You lost someone you love?"

"I did. My husband."

"I'm so sorry. I thought you said you still had a husband?" I situated myself upright in my seat and tried to piece together my suspicions of witchery.

"I do. He's alive now. You'll meet him soon. But the point is, I understand the grief you're facing," she said.

The train disappeared down the tracks with one last whistle. The barricades rose in front of us, and Fritzi stepped on the gas pedal and continued.

"Wait a minute. How is he alive? I knew it! You *are* a witch. Just admit it." I brushed an unruly lock of hair from my face and lowered my window for a blast of fresh air. The smell of wood smoke still clung to my hair, causing my stomach to grow queasy.

"Remember when I said I'd been to the magic world? My husband was a genie in Morningwood. Before I saved him." Her voice fell to an almost-inaudible pitch.

"It sounds like you have a story to tell too." I folded my arms across my chest, waiting for her next move.

"I'll tell you mine if you tell me yours." She sighed, slumping her shoulders forward.

Her posture gave away her role as the stereotypical exhausted mother, and I realized, this entire time, she'd hidden it well.

"Deal. But what's said in this car stays in this car. Or at least, if you report things, run them by me first," I said, sticking my hand out for her to shake in agreement.

"You have my word." She clasped her palm around mine and squeezed.

"All right, I'll go first. I might as well get it out now. I never want to speak about it again." I took a deep breath and pulled whatever courage I could find from wherever the hell it was hiding and began to relive the haunting misery of last night.

"Once upon a time," I began.

IT WAS NEARLY lunchtime when we arrived at Fritzi's home. A deep, gnawing hunger ached in the pit of my stomach, reminding me I'd not eaten since before the ball. My appetite had disappeared, but the ferocious growls from my stomach were relentless.

"You've got to be famished. Come on. Let's get you cleaned up, and I'll make lunch." Fritzi turned off her car and scooted out the door.

I followed behind her, stopping at the door nestled into the side of a white brick house.

She kicked a small pile of leaves aside, revealing a faded straw doormat that read, *Gangster's Paradise.*

"What's a gangster's paradise?" I asked.

"Well, my husband's a comedian. Literally, so just be fore-warned. He thought gangster's paradise was funny because our house is, um, not that at all. We have baby bottles and cribs." She paused, tapping her chin. "Yes, a crib. I guess that fits. Welcome to my crib."

She pushed her key in the door and nudged the door open, making a sweeping motion for me to enter.

"Thanks. I didn't know humans slept in cribs!" I said, stepping over the doorstep and into a hallway lined with pictures.

"That's not what I meant." She laughed, shutting the door behind us. "Never mind. What can I make you for lunch? We've got it all. My husband has a thing for junk food, so whatever you want to eat, we have it."

"Junk food?" I asked.

She rubbed a palm down her face and blinked. "I have so much to teach you. Come on. Let me show you to your room, so you can get cleaned up, and then we can explore the kitchen!"

"Do you have any coffee stuff like at The Royal Beagle?" I asked, raising my voice above the incessant groans from my belly.

"Did somebody say *junk food*? Who summoned me?" A handsome man appeared from around the corner, holding the tiniest of humans in his arms.

"I like when I summon you in other ways, but I'll let it slide since you're on baby duty. Henry, meet Penelope. Penelope, meet Henry and Elyse. We call her Elly."

Fritzi set her purse and keys down on a nearby bench and reached for her daughter. Henry quickly handed her off.

"Oh, my big blue … bells and whistles! I've never met a true princess before. It's a pleasure to meet you, Your Majesty!" Henry bowed before me. His messy hair fell across his brow, reminding me of Vail.

My vampire boyfriend had a thick head of hair, perfect for winding my fingers through and tugging as I kissed him or when his head bobbed from between my legs. The memory of Vail sent a charge of excitement between my thighs but an ache of grief through my heart.

"I'm afraid I can't call myself a princess anymore. I'm just … one of you." I curtsied.

Elly let out a coo.

"You sound so disappointed!" Henry furrowed his brow.

"As interesting as humans are, I prefer home. It's where my loved ones are … were." I hung my head. "Do you not miss the supernatural realm? Do you not miss home?"

"Your Majesty," Henry said.

"Call me Penelope." I gave him a dismissive wave.

"Penelope, my home was in a big blue dildo. I was trapped in there for longer than I care to remember. This is my home now." He swung his arm around Fritzi and pulled her close, kissing her forehead.

Elly raised her arms, reaching for her dad.

"He's charming, isn't he?" Fritzi handed Elly back to Henry and gave them each a peck on the cheek. "Come on. More chitchat later. You're caked in mud, blood, and I don't even want to know what else. Goblin goo? Troll hair? What's that smudge? A dragon shart?"

"Ba-dum-cha! She gets it from me," Henry said.

"Close. My ex-fiancé's shitty remains." I twisted my mouth into a grin.

"And we have a winner. Princess Penelope, we're going to get along just fine! Off you go. I'm going to give you a taste— literally—of what it's like to be human. They have stuff here you couldn't ever even dream of! Cronuts, bean burritos, nacho cheese, Twinkies!" Henry sang as he whisked Elly away.

"I hope his humor doesn't offend you! Henry is such a

lovable dork. You'll see. He's probably setting up a smorgasbord for you right now." Fritzi led me out of the hall and up a flight of stairs.

"Dork? Smorgasbord?" I asked, shuffling my feet up the carpeted steps.

We passed by a room filled with stuffed bookcases and a desk covered in stacks of paper.

"My office," Fritzi pointed out, reaching for the door and shutting the mess behind it. "I can't get much work done here between Elly and my nonstop talkative husband. It's why I head to The Royal Beagle for a weekend escape sometimes. Well, that, and research. It's all about the research." She winked. "Besides, there's something almost magical about that place. I always felt it, but you? You proved it! Something supernatural lurks there. I doubt magic would have taken you to the local coffee shop here. It's filled with briefcases and business suits—the exact opposite of The Royal Beagle's down-to-earth customers."

"It did feel different. Maybe because it was in Morningwood, but I felt more comfortable there than here in ... what did you call this place?" I asked.

"I picked you up in Outer Forks. But we're in Forks now." She opened the door to a small room, which was neatly decorated with cozy furnishings. The quilt atop the bed was sewn in a bright floral pattern, matching the rug beneath the bed's wooden frame.

"Forks," I repeated, walking toward the quilt and tracing my fingertips over the stitches.

"The bathroom is right there. Fresh towels are under the sink, a new toothbrush is in the drawer, and if there's anything else you need, just let me know. Oh! I'll bring a few pieces of clothes up and lay them by the door, so you can choose what you want to wear. We look like we wear the same size."

"Thank you. I appreciate you doing all of this for me. I'm kind of on autopilot right now. I'll snap out of it with time. And then I can be of more help."

"Penelope, you've been through a traumatic experience. The only thing I need from you is rest. Be easy on yourself, and when you're feeling up for it, we can try to figure your dilemma out together and then get you back to Vail. If that's what you want."

I nodded. The mere mention of his name caused tears to well in my eyes and a knot to form in my throat. I didn't trust myself to speak without letting out a wail I'd been suppressing for far too long. I wanted more than anything to collapse into his safe arms, but if I were anywhere near him, he'd become a target again.

"I'll see you in a bit." She backed out of the guest room, shutting the door behind her.

I stepped out of my dirty heels and dragged myself to the bathroom. The cold tiles on the floor sent a chill up my spine. I shivered and pulled the vinyl shower curtain to the side. The porcelain tub sparkled like new. I turned on the hot water and waited until the bathroom filled with steam, fogging up the glass on a mirror I refused to look into. I would give anything for an insult from Mirror Mirror. But instead, I would never hear that asshole's voice again.

I stepped into the tub and sat on the bottom, curling my knees to my chest and letting the hard pelts of water wash over me. Dirty water swirled down the drain, washing away someone's blood, sweat, tears, and, yeah, probably even a bit of goblin goo. I threw my head back, letting the hot water stream down my face and through my tangled hair.

I scrubbed my cheeks, my arms, and my chest until my skin turned an alarmingly raw red hue—the same violent color as the flames that licked at the wooden beams of my old burned-down cottage. I ran my fingers through my stiff hair, frantically trying to rub away any trace of last night. But no matter how rough I was with myself, I couldn't shed the memories that I knew would haunt me forever. My godmother was dead, and in a sense, so was I—gone from my home, my friends, and my lover … forever.

I buried my face in my wet hands and screamed.

CHAPTER TWO

VAIL

I SAT, DUMBFOUNDED, WATCHING PENELOPE'S COTTAGE crumble in flames until it became only a smolder. Her goat, Grump, and her enchanted Mirror Mirror insisted we leave the area at once. They both thought we were next on the hit list.

"She's not coming back, you know." Mirror Mirror sat, propped on a tree behind me, reflecting the glowing embers of what had once been his home. His voice cut through the eerie silence like a blade. It was the first time anyone had spoken.

"I know." I hung my head and scrubbed my palms over my face. A slick film of grime coated my skin, catching under my fingernails.

Grump coughed beside me, drawing my attention. Specks of ash littered the tufts of fur hanging from his snout. "Can we go now? I don't feel safe. There's nothing here anymore."

Trevor flicked his bushy foxtail in the air and moved closer to the wreckage. Otto, his gargoyle best friend, followed behind him. The gargoyle slipped in a pile of Pumpkin's guts and slid sideways toward the flames. He let out a screech and hopped back to Trevor, settling in beside him. They stubbornly refused to leave the site.

"There's nothing back at the winery anymore either. I'm sure everything's destroyed," I muttered, scuffing my foot in the dirt.

"We don't know for certain. What about your brothers? Can you tell us what happened?" Mirror Mirror asked.

I turned my head and noticed for the first time the crack stretching across his surface.

"The Council. You might know them as the overseers of the vampire world. Their mission has always been to expand vampirism. Not totally, of course. In the food chain, we're at the top. But we can't stay at the top if we don't have any prey. So, they're methodical in their wars. But when my brothers and I opened the lab, we knew we were setting out on a dangerous course. Anything that worked the opposite of expanding vampirism would be destroyed—along with us. Somehow, they found out. There's a snitch in our circle." My fangs lowered, dripping with venom.

"And so they destroyed the winery. Ugh, all that wasted wine." Grump shook his head.

"And the beasts and creatures in it. They killed my brother Leo. And who knows who else? I need to get back to survey the damage and look for clues. Someone said something. Someone knows our secret." I jumped to my feet.

The misery of the night had quickly turned to bloodlust. I would take revenge on The Council for what they'd done. But I needed to find the traitor who had tipped them off first.

"I'm so sorry. Do you think they're still there? Where will we go? What now?" Mirror Mirror asked.

I glanced up at the purple sky, growing pink around the

edges. I'd completely lost track of time. I must have spent hours staring into the flames, and I remembered none of it. The last memory I had of the night was when the woman I'd fallen for vanished in my arms, leaving me here, alone.

"No. They left a long time ago. They were only there to send a message. Luckily, they must not have known Penelope was the cure. Otherwise, they would have killed her," I choked out my words before clearing my throat.

If the vampires caught Penelope, she'd be better off dead than have to live through what they'd do to her.

"Now, we go back to the winery, survey the damage, and find the culprit. Then, I'll drain him until he's an inch within his life and inject him with enough poison to make him suffer but not turn him. I'll watch him slip away into a prolonged and torturous death. After that, I'll get back to work."

"And what about Penelope?" Grump nudged himself against my knees.

"I think she's safer outside of Morningwood. At least until I deal with The Council. I'll find her after that."

Trevor looked back at me and growled. The fur on the back of his neck stood on end. Otto tried to mimic him but instead let out a wail like a foghorn, startling himself and every creature within a two-hundred-yard radius.

"I *will* find her," I said in a firm and final voice.

"And we'll help." Mirror Mirror sighed as I heaved him into my arms and carried him through the forest and back to Bostwick.

Grump trotted behind us, but Trevor and Otto refused to budge.

"What's a mirror going to do? Reflect my good looks back to me?" I tried to lighten the mood, suppressing my aching, nonexistent heart in the empty chambers of my chest.

It wasn't long ago that I'd felt my first heartbeat. I didn't

17

know how to explain it or if it meant there was a piece of heart tissue left in there. But I knew it was because of Penelope—and not just because her blood could cure my vampire disease. She brought me to life too. The magnetism of her smile, the soft curves of her body, and the slow, drugging, dizzying kisses we shared all beckoned me under her spell. The princess had charmed me like no other woman I'd ever encountered.

"You underestimate me. Look," Mirror Mirror said, drawing my attention back to him. His face disappeared as he showed me the inside of a shop.

"What's that?" I paused, staring into the familiar diner.

"The Royal Beagle. The coffee shop Penelope always disappeared to."

I held the mirror out, studying his reflection. A waitress in a stained pink apron dragged her feet through the front door, ringing the bell.

"Another day, another dollar," she said, flicking on the lights.

"Can they see us?" I whispered.

"No. They can't hear you either. There was a reason Penelope always ended up at The Royal Beagle. It's not the typical human coffee shop. I'm pretty sure it's witchowned or something. I didn't think to check there until after she said the name of the place the last time she vanished."

"So, if she always went there before, she must be there now?" I asked, watching the waitress brew a pot of coffee.

An older man pushed open the door, ringing the bell again. His nose stuck out from his face in a bony hook. He made his way behind the counter and tied an apron around his neck, pausing slightly to cock his head toward the mirror —toward us.

"She's not. I checked as soon as she left. I'm sorry." Mirror

Mirror's face faded back into view as The Royal Beagle disappeared.

"Thanks, Mirror Mirror. I think you will definitely prove useful. You can explain more once we get settled back at the winery." I rushed us out of the woods and through the vineyards while the sun began to crest. My skin started to tingle.

"What can I do?" Grump shouted, barely able to keep up. He scurried behind us as he hoofed it as quick as his fat, little legs could run.

"You can ..." I racked my brain for a task for the drunk but tenderhearted goat. "You can help the brothers in the vineyard. We'll need to keep tending the vines," I said as I reached the ballroom and stopped, taking a deep breath to prepare myself for the carnage inside.

I turned my face back toward the woods, where only a faint trail of smoke curled over the treetops.

"I *will* find her," I said under my breath. I pivoted on my heels and opened the ballroom's grand doors, stepping into a scene from hell.

"VAIL!" Priscilla gathered her dress in her fists and ran toward me, stopping me at the door. Ash, blood, and a hint of unease dulled her usual dewy glow.

"Are you all right?" I asked.

"Where is she? Where is she?!" Priscilla's voice rose into a shrill.

"Who? Penelope?"

"Yes! Where's the princess?"

"Gone. Faded. Out of my reach." I hung my head. "The cottage burned down ... with Gertie in it. Penelope couldn't get there in time to save her. But she saw the blue smoke and vanished."

Priscilla shifted her weight on her feet and looked away. Her inky-black eyes flashed like a spark of fire in the dead of night.

"She tried to save her?" she spat out. The edge in her voice cut like steel. Her expression grew into a mask of stone.

"Yeah, she tried. I tried. We were too late." I held up my palm and shrugged.

She opened her mouth to speak but stopped herself. "Never mind."

She turned on her heels and marched out the door, disappearing in a dizzying whirlwind. The breeze from her spell slapped me across the face like a whip.

"That lady gives me the creeps," Grump said.

"She does that to everyone," I replied.

I stepped into the ballroom. The air was filled with the metallic scent of fresh blood. The intoxicating aroma set my fangs on edge. I'd not fed on blood since Penelope let me drink from her. Nothing compared to the taste of her blood on my tongue, and after one sip of her, human blood had lost its enticement. I wrinkled my nose and stepped over a dead body the size of a football.

"Poor gnome," I sighed, forcing myself to look away from his vacant eyes and twisted jaw.

I searched the ballroom for my brothers. Drake sat on the opposite side of the room with his head in his hands. His clothes hung in tatters around his frame. It seemed like only yesterday, my youngest brother had volunteered to turn vampire and help our cause—as long as he wasn't sworn to turn back into his human self once we found the cure.

He'd spent his short life running, conning, manipulating. In the human world, those skills had only gotten him into trouble more often than not. But he was talented, and he wanted to use his talent freely. When a chance encounter with Leo had led to his decision to turn, he'd become our number one asset—until Penelope.

Drake lured humans to us in ways I couldn't imagine. His charm, charisma, and manipulative skills conned even the brightest of people. He'd once convinced a heart surgeon to come in for a wine tasting. The surgeon had left with a buzz, and we'd harvested a great deal of his DNA and his knowledge without him knowing.

I set Mirror Mirror on a nearby table and told Grump to stay with him. Glass shards from our chandelier littered the wooden floor. The massive fixture had fallen, shattering into a thousand pieces across where Penelope and I had danced only hours ago. I maneuvered around a pile of ash, wondering if the vampire it belonged to was from The Council.

"He's not handling it so well, is he?" I tipped my head at Drake as I walked toward Ian.

Ian's face drooped. Dry blood was caked across his hairline and spattered over his white button-up. He lazily swept the floor, moving pieces of bone and debris toward the corner of the room.

"He thought the vamp life was glamorous. Can't say we didn't warn him." Ian's voice came out in a long and solemn drawl.

The remaining unbroken lights flickered overhead.

"What about Finn? Where is he?"

"Went down to check the labs. Said he's sure as shit they destroyed that too. But he ain't been back since." He wiped his arm across his face, smearing a streak of soot over his jaw.

"Brother, get some sleep. I'd say you look like death, but that doesn't mean anything to a vampire. So, instead, I'll say you look like yourself, only an ancient and ugly version." I

21

squeezed his shoulder. "The sun's already up. We can take care of this when we wake."

"Leo would want to finish it now. He'd say we're at war. This is our battlefield. And—"

"And he isn't here. Look at our brother." I motioned toward Drake. "Have you seen him like that? He's in shock. We can't let this destroy us. Leo would want us collected to finish our mission."

"And to also finish our battle."

"And finish our battle," I agreed. "But we can't do it in exhaustion. Grab a Project X and go to bed. We'll meet back here at dusk. I'm going to check on Finn. Maybe you can get Drake out of here too."

Ian released the broom from his grip, letting it fall to the floor in a crash, which echoed throughout the ballroom. I turned away from the shredded curtains, the broken tables, and my devastated brothers.

Grump and Mirror Mirror were having an animated conversation where I'd left them. The goat picked up a bottle of wine between his teeth and tossed it back. The red liquid ran down the sides of his snout, coating his beard in the color of blood.

"I'm going to get those two up to my room before they make more trouble for us."

"Oh. Why are they here and not with Penelope?" he asked.

I shook my head, brushing my unruly hair from my brow. "She's gone. But I can't explain right now. I need to see what happened to the lab. Her blood ... I need to see if there's any of it left."

"Why her blood?" He rubbed his tired eyes and yawned. His fangs were stained red.

"It's special," I whispered, narrowing my eyes and hoping he'd get the point not to probe any further. "Really, really special. Like a breakthrough special."

"Oh." A sudden look of realization crossed his face. "So, that's why they did all this." He rubbed the back of his neck and stared at the ground.

"Not exactly. They don't know about her. Otherwise, they'd have left no trace of her on earth. She's just in the human realm for now. And that's classified information for you. Not for Drake. Not yet anyway. Someone tipped them off about our labs. We need to find out who before we can move on. But I need to find Penelope too. Then, maybe we can get back to the project and deal with The Council."

"I'm so sorry, Vail. We'll get her back. And we'll get these bastards back for what they did. For Leo, for us, for the cause. For the right to choose between curing our disease or living with it. Fuck those assholes who did this." Ian's voice deepened into a growl. "Whoever ratted us out is going to pay for this. I'll make damn sure of it."

"Shh. We can't let this get out. Keep your eyes open and stay on guard. I'll see you in a bit." I backed away from Ian and tried to give him a look of reassurance. But his gaze was transfixed on Drake.

"Gee, boss. This place is going to need a lot of work." Grump hiccuped while chewing the side of a tablecloth.

I scooped Mirror Mirror in my arms and motioned for the goat to follow. We wound our way through carnage before heading toward the hallway in the back, leading into the main home.

"Yeah, but it's not important now. Let's get you two settled. I've got one more thing to check on before I have to get some rest. Mirror Mirror, did you recheck The Royal Beagle?"

"Aye. No sign of turd muffin," he replied.

I cleared my throat. "Come again?"

"It's a term of endearment. Really. The princess isn't at the coffee shop. I've checked several times, and I'll continue.

I'm also checking a few other mirrors where I have connections. And I've spread the word that there's a royal nutbag on the loose."

"If I didn't know you were secretly very fond of Penelope, I'd throw you in the pond out back. But thanks for the help, I guess. Where're the other mirrors?" I stared down at my reflection, which quickly transformed into various flashing scenes.

"My reach doesn't travel very far, but I can drop in on this bookshop. It's in another city called Forks," he said before showing me another location. "There's also one in a chapel in the woods. I've no idea where. That's it as far as I know."

"Interesting. I never knew there was a network of mirrors. Are they enchanted? As in can someone look at the mirror in the bookshop and see what we're doing?" My heels echoed down the empty corridor.

Hours ago, this place had thrived with life, and now, the winery had turned into one giant graveyard.

"Nope. I'm the only soul trapped inside the network. I'm one of a kind!"

The goat let out a guffaw and fell over on his side in a series of twitches.

"Damn it!" I stopped to hoist him under my other arm. His rounded belly sagged under my palm.

"Stupid, drunk goat." Mirror Mirror rolled his eyes.

I huffed as I carried them both up the creaky stairs and into my room. I kept my eyes focused straight ahead, refusing to look at Leo's door or push it open to see how he'd left it. I already knew. His bed would be made in strict, formal military-style. His shoes would lay tucked neatly at the end. Everything would be tidy and in order, and the scent of his old-man aftershave would still be lingering on his pillow.

I swallowed hard. The goat hung limp in my arm, already

passed out. But Mirror Mirror kept talking, distracting me from the grief I pushed down deep inside of me, locking it away somewhere I dared not venture.

"I mean, I don't want to be a jerk. I try not to—sometimes. The only love I had was Gertie. She talked to me like … like I was a part of something more, like a part of the family. Penelope didn't see me that way though. I think Penelope blamed me for pissing off Theo too much and playing a part in him banishing us," he said.

"Well, you don't have to worry about Theo anymore."

Mirror Mirror's face lit up into a shine. "I thought I recognized his fat head rolling around back there. Hmmph. It serves him right. Even dead, he was still wearing a dumb look on his face. Karma, I'm tellin' you."

"Karma," I echoed. I hadn't known Theo personally, but I felt no remorse for any man who could treat Penelope the way he had. "I'm sorry about Gertie. She was an extraordinary woman."

"Yes, she was. One toss of her wand, and she'd fix this unsightly crack across my face. I guess it's my battle scar now. I'm just lucky that dumbass gargoyle was there to carry me out. I didn't see a thing. I was in the other room. But I felt the heat of the fire. That's all I remember."

"We'll fix your face. No worries. I'm glad Otto was there too. Maybe he and Trevor will come around before too long. But I have a feeling they'll not wander far from what's left of the cottage. They're waiting on Penelope to come back." I nudged the door open with my foot and carried Grump to the rug at the end of my bed. I didn't want to sleep with a smelly goat tonight. My gaze raked over a hairbrush full of golden-blonde locks left on my nightstand.

"Thanks, Vail." Mirror Mirror's voice came out low, as if he'd had to force out his words.

"For?" I asked.

"For not leaving me behind."

I carried him over to a lone nail hanging on my wooden clapboard wall and hooked him over the top of it, securing him until I made sure he was steady enough to hang.

"You're a part of Penelope's family, which makes you a part of mine now too." I tried to smile, but the grief I'd kept pushing down inside of me was slowly making its way back up. I rubbed my empty chest and left without saying another word.

Mirror Mirror suppressed a sniffle as I shut the door behind me.

THE SCENT of bleach mixed with blood caught me off guard as I reached the underground lab. Broken bottles were scattered across the floor, and congealed blood was splattered over the stark white tiles. Gallons of bleach lay turned over, flooding half the room in a dizzying aroma. I sank my foot into the mixture of chemicals and our precious harvested DNA and made my way to Finn's back office. The liquid immediately soaked through my shoes.

"Finn?" I called, dodging a halogen lamp swinging lopsided from the ceiling.

The light flickered twice before sputtering out.

I scanned the lab for signs of my brother and any salvageable materials. Neither existed.

"Finn?" I called again.

An uneasy feeling spread across my chest. This laboratory was Finn's life. The Council had destroyed his entire life's work. I shuffled my feet toward the cooling chamber that stored Penelope's blood. A scratching sound, followed by a loud crash, came from the ground beneath me.

My fangs lowered, and my senses heightened. I wasn't alone.

"Who's there?" I growled, backing myself into a corner.

A pile of stakes sat in a thick gray puddle beside the far wall. The tiles surrounding it were streaked black with ash. I narrowed my vision toward the pile, trying to understand what had happened and where it had come from, but an unfamiliar hiss of escaped air rang out into the empty room. Finn's desk moved to the side as he crawled out from underneath it.

"What the hell?" I stared at him in disbelief.

"They didn't get it. They thought they did! But damn it, those bastards aren't as smart as they think they are!" Finn cackled. His hair stuck out wildly from his thin face.

"Where exactly did you come from? What's down there? Why didn't I know about it?" I inched toward my brother, peering over his desk and into a black hole.

"No one knew but me. Do you think I spent all my time down here, playing with the lab equipment? No!" He shook his head. "I saved it. All of it." His eyes grew wide, bordering on maniacal.

"The DNA samples?"

"Yes. Among other … projects." He closed the trapdoor and slid under his desk, punching his fingers at something stuck to the underside of the desktop. With eight beeps, the trapdoor locked with a click.

I rubbed my jaw and tried to make sense of what was happening, but my exhaustion got the best of me.

"I'm tired. I can't take in any more information. Just tell me, we're good? Anything I need to know? You still have Penelope's blood, right?"

He marched to the other side of the room, flinging his lab coattails to the side.

27

"The princess's blood is safe. Why do you ask? Where is she?" He pivoted on his heels, turning to face me.

"Gone. She faded."

"What?" He curled his fists to his sides. "Where did she fade to? We must get her at once! I have plenty of her … DNA … but she's the backup plan too. We'll eventually run out of her blood. Without it, we're a lost cause. Fucking Council!" he hissed, baring his fangs.

"I'll find her. But first, I need to find the traitor who tipped The Council off about our little project, and we need to get things cleaned and back up and running. If I brought Penelope back now, she'd be in danger. We'll deal with the traitor first."

"So, we have a traitor among us? Shit. I'm not sure we have the time to deal with that before finding Penelope and getting her someplace safe."

"What do you mean?"

"The goo over there," he said, snapping his eyes to the pile of stakes. "That was a vampire I killed. He tried to set the place on fire. But before that, he drank a few vials of blood. One of them, Penelope's. You should have seen his face once a drop of her blood hit his lips."

"But he's dead."

Finn looked away. "After he took a sip, he read the label aloud and passed it to his friend. I was in *my* secret lab when all this happened, watching from that camera." He tilted his head toward a camera in the corner.

"Fuck." I ran my hands through my hair and steadied myself against a wall.

"So, they know Penelope's blood is at least part of the cure. I was only quick enough to kill one. The other one ran," he said.

"That's why they burned down her cottage." I swallowed hard.

The heavy scent of chemicals suddenly weighed on me, causing me to stumble into a nearby cabinet. A few empty bottles fell from the top, crashing to the floor in a hundred tiny pieces.

"Fuck! Fuck! Fuck!" I yelled. "So, she's in danger now. They know. Fuck! I have to find her ASAP."

"I'm sorry, brother."

"Is there anything you can do to help me find her? Run some numbers on something? Use some data? I don't know much about the human world. I try to stay away from it."

His eyes flickered to his smashed laptop. The keys lay scattered across the top of his desk.

"I'll do what I can. I've copies of everything down there." He motioned toward the trapdoor. "I'll help when I can, but go save the princess first. Then, we can come up with a plan to find the traitor and deal with The Council. I have no idea how we'll take them on. We'll need an army to defeat those bastards."

"An army. Leo's army," I sighed. "Wish he were here to see it."

Finn hung his head. "His legacy will live on forever. When we roll out our cure, he'll go down in history as the founder."

"And you'll go down in history as the one who made it all happen. That was very smart of you to create ... whatever it is down there." I pressed my lips into a thin line and then forced myself to say the words I needed to say in case I lost another loved one before I could tell them they mattered, "You're a brilliant scientist, and I'm proud to call you my brother."

"Same to you, Vail." His voice wavered.

I left, overtaken with the misery of the night. My brain drained of all thoughts and emotions, and my weary body switched to autopilot.

"Just one thing," he called out after me.

"Yeah?" I asked.

"Don't tell anyone—and I mean, anyone—about my secret lab. Okay? Even Leo had no clue. The fewer people who know, the better."

"Your secret is safe with me." I touched my forehead slightly in a mock salute and made my way out of the room and back into bed.

Grump and Mirror Mirror were in a deep snooze. The goat lay on his back with all four hooves in the air.

I settled into bed and dozed off quickly.

But before too long, I awoke again in the middle of a nightmare. I tossed and turned to dreams of roaring fires, deathly screams, and an eerie black hole beneath my brother's desk.

CHAPTER THREE

PENELOPE

THE SCENT OF COFFEE PULLED ME OUT OF MY BED AND INTO
the kitchen. I'd spent the last several days sleeping, sobbing,
and reliving memories, so I could put the puzzle pieces
together and move forward. Details of the massacre were
foggy, and I needed to understand how the events had played
out. I needed to finish what the vampires had started.
Vengeance had always been my fatal flaw.

Night terrors kept me awake most of the night, and
during the day, Henry's forced food comas kept me in a deep
slumber. I knowingly suspended myself in a constant state of
agony, despair, and semiconsciousness, rifling through my
thoughts and filing away crucial details. I wrote down bits of
information that came to me in clarity but quickly fled my
memory, as if my brain could protect itself from the scent of
burning vampires or the entrails of a werewolf tangled
around my slipper.

I couldn't let go, and I couldn't move on until I had
closure, but I'd get it one way or another. The only reason I

dragged myself down the stairs this morning was because my desire for vengeance overshadowed my need to grieve. I couldn't waste away in bed all day. I had to act.

"Good morning, sunshine!" Henry flashed by me in an instant, holding out a steaming mug of coffee.

"Thanks," I mumbled, cupping the warm mug between my palms. I stuck my nose over the rim, took a deep breath, and sighed.

"Who needs magic when you have coffee?" He wiggled his brows before returning to the refrigerator and opening its door. He stuck his head inside and began to hum.

I walked past a sink full of dirty dishes and made my way toward Elly, sitting in a chair buckled atop another chair across from Fritzi. A scattering of crumbs, crusts, and mashed vegetables decorated the floor beneath the baby's seat.

"Feeling better?" Fritzi asked, eyeing my choice of clothes.

Since I'd arrived, all I'd worn was an oversize navy-blue shirt lined with wool and topped with a floppy hood. Dresses and anything pink no longer fit my mood, and this man top had become the perfect place to hide. It even had pockets.

"A bit." I set the mug down on the water-stained table and pulled out a chair, settling in beside Elly.

She held out her hands and curled her palms in my direction, hopping in her seat.

"Aw. Look at that! She's already a fan of the princess. She wants you to hold her!" Fritzi said. She gently placed her fingertips to her heart and cooed before giving Elly a playful bop on the nose.

"Me? I've not—I mean, I'm not ..." I stuttered.

I'd never held a baby before. I didn't have much experience with children because childrearing wasn't a requirement in princess school. It wasn't possible for a princess to birth children. Instead, we *grew* children in a Princess

Patch, and godmothers helped us raise them—if we were lucky.

Princess Patches were rare, and there wasn't exactly a secret formula to planting one. They just happened, with or without sowing magic seeds. But if I ever wanted to make a name for myself as a queen, I'd at least have to give growing a Princess Patch a shot. Not that I didn't want to plant babies. I loved kids. Really. I thought I did anyway. I hadn't been taught anything about parenting or birth, so when it came down to it, I was clueless—and a little bit terrified.

The only thing I knew about motherhood was how exhausting it could be. Gertie had made sure to hammer that thought in my brain every chance she could. She told me mothers always worried and never slept. My godmother made parenting sound downright miserable—mostly anyway. She couldn't explain the motherly love and natural instincts that came with the gift of motherhood, as she called it. She'd said it was inexplicable and that I'd have to truly find out for myself one day because it was like magic no one could re-create.

I'd had no idea what she meant. But after spending a moment watching Fritzi make the sound of a train whistle while shoving a tiny spoon in her daughter's mouth and giggling, I thought I could one day learn what my godmother had tried to explain.

As for the birthing part of motherhood, I would never understand it. I didn't know how humans and other creatures violently birthed their spawn and then chose to do it over and over again. It was all crazy to me. If I had to push anything the size of Elly from between my legs, I was confident it would kill my desire for motherhood altogether. And that was only the beginning of mom life.

"Have you never held a baby before?" Fritzi asked, unbuckling Elly.

The child waved her hands in the air and bounced.

"Course she hasn't! She's a princess. They have wet nurses and peasants for that kind of stuff. Right?" Henry asked, carrying over a greasy cardboard box and plopping it on the table in front of me.

Elly squealed and pointed at the box.

"No, ma'am. You're not eating pizza! You can have more bananas or oatmeal but not junk. Your dad is such a terrible influence." Fritzi wiped Elly's face and delicately picked her up from the chair, as if she'd plucked a flower. She settled the wiggly girl on her lap.

"I don't know much about babies. She sure is cute though." I pushed my back into the chair, farther away from mom and daughter.

"Holding a baby is like holding a burrito! They're soft and squishy and full of magic and—fair warning—gas." Henry flipped open the box's lid and took out a slice of bread with what looked like cheese and vegetables mixed with some type of round red sausage slices.

"I think I'd rather hold that, to be honest." I eyed the food but winked at Elly. I couldn't allow myself to get close to anyone else, especially before I left.

"Oh yeah! Me too." Henry smacked his lips. "Kidding. I love my daughter. But cold pizza? Dude, that's where it's at. It's basically a human staple for breakfast. You don't get your human card until you've tried this. I ordered it last night for this morning's breakfast. I'm trying to teach you the finer things in life, Princess. You know, other than royal balls and crystal slippers."

"I'll try it, but I don't want my human card. Actually, I wanted to speak with you two about that today." I scooped a slice of cold pizza into my hand and took a bite. A burst of flavor danced across my tongue. I took another bite and another.

"See? Thinking twice about your human card now." Henry walked back toward the kitchen sink. His shoes flashed bright with each step.

"Maybe. Are you making sparks? I thought there was no magic here?" I asked, eyeing my next slice.

Elly grunted and wiggled in Fritzi's arms until Fritzi tore off a piece of pizza crust and handed it to her daughter. The little girl gripped it in her palm and gummed it down into a slobbery pulp.

"Ah. These bad boys?" He stuck his foot in the air, twisting his ankle from side to side. "It's another cool human thing you don't get to see in the magic world. These are my light-up shoes. Every time I step, they light up!" He hopped up and down, his shoes flashing on each bounce. "I usually stash them under my bed and only put them on at night when I have to run to the potty. That way, I can see at night. Brilliant, eh?"

Elly pointed her crust at her dad and opened her mouth into a wide, toothless grin before bursting into giggles. The sound of her laughter sent a twitch through my ovaries.

"Oh my gosh!" Fritzi beamed. "She's never laughed like that before. Do it again, Henry!"

Henry bounced on his feet, slinging his arms around in a funny dance. The child threw her head back in contagious laughter. I dropped my cold pizza on the table and gripped my sides as I watched dad and daughter's silly exchange. I laughed at their antics with tears streaming down my face, forgetting—for a quick moment—why I was here.

"The things we do for love," Fritzi said, breaking the spell and rising from the table.

My smile faded as quickly as it had come.

Fritzi handed Elly to Henry and pushed the lever on the sink, turning on the water and filling a small cup. She busied herself with watering a dead houseplant sitting on the window ledge. It was far too gone for her to save, but she watered it anyway.

I hid my trembling lips in my mug, quickly sipping the hot coffee down and scalding my taste buds. Elly and Henry had both tired out and returned to shoveling food in their mouths.

I cleared my throat before speaking again, "So, I was thinking. Can you take me back to Bostwick? I need to find Vail and let him know I'm all right. He mentioned before that he doesn't like to venture very far from Morningwood. He's not comfortable around humans. I guess they make him … hungry." I swung my legs back and forth beneath my chair, scuffing my feet across the linoleum.

My pulse quickened at my lie, but I needed revenge like I needed another slice of pizza. It was happening, no matter who got in my way. At least Fritzi and Henry would believe I only wanted to travel back to Morningwood for Vail.

"I'm going to take a wild guess that he's probably out searching for you now. Though I don't know how far vampires can get since they're restricted to night travel. I can't say I know much about them or any creatures that straddle both worlds, except for genies. I stayed shackled to my dildo in Morningwood for far too long. Everything I know has been mostly through what Fritzi's learned and Abe's Book Emporium." He shrugged.

"What's Abe's Book Emporium?" I asked, finishing my last sip of coffee.

"A bookshop in Outer Forks. They specialize in the creepy stuff. I'm pretty sure the owner is a wizard, though he'd never admit it. But those publications in there aren't all written by humans. I even came across a book on marketing that I swear was written by an ogre. He even spelled out *grobel, grobel*. The gnomes do it too. I've seen a handful of tiny books in their language."

Henry smoothed his daughter's hair back with his free hand and bounced her on his hip. She gave a long blink before resting her head on his shoulder. She stubbornly clung to the crust until her eyes slid shut and her palm opened, dropping the food to the floor in a mess of crumbs.

Fritzi shook her head and walked toward a round black disk nestled in a bare corner. The top of the contraption blinked a dim green light under a thin layer of dust.

"I've done a lot of signings and work there. The old wizard isn't fooling anyone. And considering the written word straddles realms, you know half those books in there are from fantastical places. How else do these magical beings from Morningwood find me?" she said before pushing on the top of the disk. The machine powered up in a low hum.

"What the heck is that?" I asked, curling my feet under my bottom and out of the way.

"It's my magic broom!" Fritzi laughed.

The magic broom let out a loud whirring noise and spun away from the wall. It rolled around the room the same way my poor, smashed, pervy Pumpkin used to roll around. Except this machine proved actually useful, whereas my godmother's pumpkin had not been. Fritzi's magic broom hovered atop Elly's mess, vanishing crumbs and bits of food before my eyes.

"Voilà. Magic." Henry danced around the kitchen, holding Elly tight to his chest.

The baby still slept. Her long lashes swept across the top of her rosy cheeks. She looked so peaceful and innocent while she dozed, and I had the sudden urge to hold her. I shook the thought from my head and watched the magic broom circle the table, leaving the floor spotless.

"I think if you want to get back to Vail, we need to go about it the right way. I don't feel like it's safe in Morningwood right now. Not yet anyway. What about The Council?" Fritzi asked, turning my attention back to the conversation.

The mere mention of The Council caused my pulse to rise again. I wondered if Vail could feel my heartbeat through dimensions.

"They probably think they've done their part and will leave Bostwick alone now. I'm not sure they know I'm the key to ending them. Otherwise, I'd be dead." I swallowed hard. "That's another reason I need to go. I don't want to put you all in danger."

Henry sucked in a harsh breath through his teeth and cradled Elly's head to his chest. "You're right. We can't let anyone know you're here. If they find out you're a danger to them, they'll storm my home and attack my family. I'm not the genie I used to be. I have zero powers. Zilch. Nada. None. I can't protect us with just my big-ass biceps. Not against a vampire or an entire flock of them. Or whatever it would be called. A team? A school? An army? An army!"

Fritzi bit her lip and glanced at her daughter.

"I don't want to hurt anyone. If you want me to go …" I wrung my hands. I had no home, no cash, no car, and even no clothes. I had nothing in this world.

"No. You stay. We'll have to plan the Bostwick trip quickly and carefully. We can't just barge back into Morningwood without a solid plan. Someone could be there, waiting for you. The first place they'll look is at your boyfriend's winery. Let's go to Abe's and see what we can find out about The Council," Fritzi said.

She took a step toward Henry and put her hand on his back before rubbing her palm over his shoulder. His face grew slack as the tension visibly melted from him.

"Okay. But how will I get to the bookstore if I'm to remain hidden?" I asked.

"I have the perfect disguise." Henry perked up. A mischievous grin played across his lips as he handed the sleeping baby off to Fritzi and ran upstairs.

Fritzi rolled her eyes and sighed. "Here we go."

I SCOOTED DOWN, sliding my thighs over the sticky leather backseat. My ribboned skirt spread out around me, barely hiding my panties underneath. I crossed my arms over my chest and tried to hide my breasts, which were spilling out over the costume's plunging neckline.

"This is so undignified." I blew out a breath and slumped further into my seat.

"It's all we had! Well, that's not true. I have a duck costume. But I thought you might like this better. The other one smells like spoiled nachos. I bought it off a fast-food worker twirling a sign on the street corner. Best twenty I ever spent. Elly loves that costume. But this one is better for you. With your pixie wig and those pointed ears, you look nothing like a princess—just one super-hot fairy," Henry said, turning in his seat and grinning.

For a fleeting moment, I thought I caught a spark in his eye.

"He has a thing for fairies. Specifically green ones." Fritzi rolled her eyes, gripping the steering wheel until her knuckles turned white.

The car hit a bump in the road, jostling the bells on my shoes and filling the vehicle with a joyless ringing.

"This is a sex costume?" I took a piece of ribbon from my skirt and held it between my thumb and index finger before letting it fall back down. "You played dress-up in this and did it, didn't you?" My nose wrinkled at Fritzi.

"Don't kink-shame us! Besides, Fritzi cleaned it," Henry said. "I think."

39

Fritzi ignored our banter and sniffled, wiping her hand across her wet face. Ever since she'd dropped Elly off at the babysitter, she'd been tearing up with mom guilt. At least, my godmother had called it that.

One time, Gertie had pushed me to attend a dinner with a newly available prince who had supposedly traveled from far away. I wasn't interested because I'd never even heard of the man before, but she promised the experience would at least be good for me. After countless hours of listening to the prince drone on and on about himself, the night ended with his cover blown—literally.

The longer he talked, the more his head grew until his wig popped off the top of his noggin like a cork on Bostwick's most refined bubbly. After he revealed his shiny, fat head, the rest of him quickly disintegrated. I sat in front of a man more wrinkled than the tips of my toes after a long bath. It turned out, this prince was just a dirty old man, and his shitty magic had worn off quicker than expected. Once his jowls sagged down to his dinner plate, I was out. For years, Gertie had told me she still felt mom guilt over it, and from then on, she'd better screened my suitors.

"Just how am I supposed to act with this thing on anyway? Like, I'm here for what? A party?" I asked, tugging at my pointed silicone ear.

"You're Henry's new intern … er, sidekick … er, what do comedians have?" Fritzi glanced over at her husband before returning her eyes to the road ahead.

"Sideshow!" He clapped his hands. "You're the new sideshow, and we're doing a skit on supernatural stuff. Seems legit. I mean, the owner knows me. I doubt he'd question it. I'm kind of known for my wild side." He tossed his head, dramatically flinging a lock of hair from his face.

"I don't know any comedy. You don't think he'll ask me for a joke, do you?"

"No. Abe keeps to himself mostly. He'll direct us where we need to go," Henry said before jolting upright. "Oh! Oh! And where we need to go is in that direction!" He pointed out the window toward a large pink truck with a triangular-shaped object on the roof.

"Really? You just ate!" Fritzi slowed the car.

"I can't *not* stop at The Pink Taco Truck, lady. Pull over." He stuck his hand out, bracing himself against the dashboard as Fritzi swerved toward the truck.

I reached for the seat in front of me and held on tight. "What's a pink taco truck?" I asked, digging my heels into the floor to stop from falling over onto my side.

"Only the best tacos ever." He bounced in his seat, much like his tiny mini me, Elly, had done at breakfast.

"Okay. What's a taco?"

As Fritzi skidded to a halt behind the truck, he turned to look at me and covered his mouth with his palm. "I forgot they don't have those where you're from! Wow. What a sad existence. Are you sure you want to go back to that place?"

I nodded. "Nothing will keep me from Vail, and nothing will keep me from vengeance. Not even a pink taco."

"A taco is a bunch of fillings stuffed into a foldy thing. You turn your head and eat it like this." He tilted his head and stuffed his curled palm into his mouth. "And once it's in there, it all falls apart. But that's the fun part. You have another taco underneath it, waiting on the plate to catch all the good stuff. Rinse, repeat. Until you just have a plate of meat and taco shells and whatever else you want. Then, you can funnel it into your mouth like a boss. Let me demonstrate!"

"Sounds complicated," I muttered.

Henry hopped from the car and jogged toward the truck. A lady stuck her head out of the truck's side window and waved to Fritzi before noticing me and my big-ass wings sitting in the back.

"What the hell is that?" she called out to us.

Two other ladies peeked their heads out the window, too, scrunching their brows.

Fritzi rolled down her window and shouted, "What? I couldn't hear you."

"I said, what the hell is that?" The woman motioned toward her back before flinging her arms out wide, flapping them, and then pointing to me.

"Henry will explain. It's his new … sideshow. Meet Penel—I mean, Pansy," Fritzi yelled, giving the women a dismissive wave.

"Pansy?" I whispered. "I'm not a pansy! I'm a sunflower!" I brushed a fuzzball off my knee and sat up straight.

"Hush. You're a sideshow today," Fritzi said out of the corner of her mouth.

The woman in the truck nodded like she understood and turned her attention to Henry.

"We can stay parked here after we eat. The bookstore is right around the corner anyway." She shut the car off and unbuckled her seat belt before looking at the empty car seat next to me. Her bottom lip trembled.

"She'll be okay," I assured her. "Elly's probably safer at the babysitter's anyway. Since, you know, I'm with you." I let my gaze fall to my lap and began to pull at a loose thread on my skirt.

"I know. I just miss her. It's crazy how that works. One minute, I need a break, and the next, I miss her."

Henry opened the car door and slid back inside, interrupting our profound moment with his playful presence. Besides his striking good looks, I could see why Fritzi kept him around. He was the literal comedic relief to her life.

"Hey! Hey! I got us manna from the gods! Now, follow my

lead if you want to learn the secrets of the taco." Henry handed us each a handful of foil packages.

He unraveled his food and slowly twisted it into his mouth, all while holding it over his other taco and letting the filling fall to the foil on his lap.

"See? Genius," he said between chews. "I taught myself that. I guess you could say it's magic. Even Fritzi never thought about my trick before. She wasted so much food! Letting her tacos fall apart and throwing the crumbs away. That was, like, half a meal gone to waste! Ugh! It's a travesty."

"So sad." Fritzi shook her head at her taco before taking a bite.

I mimicked them, stuffing the shell into my mouth and letting half of it crumble below. The taste of this taco thing took my mind away from my dorky debut as Sideshow Pansy. My mouth watered for more as I gobbled up not two, not three, but four tacos before I paused long enough to catch my breath and then shoveled down what bits of taco were left on the foil.

Henry stared at me, wide-eyed. "Holy shit. You tore into that like an ogre in heat!"

"I guess I was hungry." I shrugged, rubbing my belly.

"Now, you're living life. Wait until you try a Mack Daddy!" He danced in his seat.

"Big Mac," Fritzi corrected him.

"Whatever. You'll love it," he said.

They crumpled their trash and stuffed it back into the bag, reaching for my wrapping and tossing it in with the other garbage.

"Let's go. I don't like leaving Elly long," Fritzi said, wiping her face with a napkin before getting out of the car.

Henry and I opened our doors and followed her out. I pushed my heels in the ground and groaned, rising to my feet. The weight of the grease I'd inhaled hung heavy in my stomach.

I dragged myself up the empty street, passing the ladies inside The Pink Taco Truck. They stared out the window as I maneuvered myself behind Fritzi, blocking their view. But it was useless. My skirt flew out behind me like a flag signaling my arrival. This costume attracted more attention than it disguised my identity.

We rounded a corner into an alleyway littered with tinted glass bottles and an overfilled trash bin near the back. Two scraggly rats sat at the bottom of the dumpster, fighting over a bone. I shivered and continued down the sloped brick path until we reached an arched doorway with only the words *Abe's Book Emporium* written on a sign above it.

"Why's it hidden back here? You'd think a bookshop would be on a busy street to attract customers." I looked from one alley to the other.

"When you read some of the books inside this place, I think you'll find Abe doesn't want to attract too many customers. Or at least, not any normal customers." Henry reached for the door, pulled it open, and stepped inside.

The scent of parchment and candlewax filled the air inside the dimly lit shop. Crystals hung above the doorframes and lay spread atop the front counter. The table at the entrance was piled high with yellow-paged books. I picked one up and peeled back the cover, breathing in the dusty-scented pages. Fritzi trailed behind me, running her fingertips along the spines of the hardbacks perched atop the cramped wooden shelves.

"Abe," Henry called.

I plucked another book from the top of a stack and thumbed through it before putting it back down. The pages left a powdery film of dust on my fingertips.

"Abe," Henry called again.

"Maybe he's in the back," Fritzi said, strolling past me. Her shoes tapped lightly, creaking across the planked floor.

Henry faced the back of the shop and scratched his head.

"Come on." Fritzi motioned for me to follow her.

We made our way through winding paths lined with narrow shelves stuffed with books. No signs directed us to genre, subjects, or hints of any organization. But the deeper into the shop we traveled, the larger the texts became. I paused, hoisting a title-less leather-bound book into my arms and flipping it over to the back cover.

"To mate a giant, you must begin to—" I said.

"Pass." Henry shuffled his feet behind me.

I cringed, swiftly placing it back where it belonged.

"Oh! What's this?" He plucked a book from a shelf. "How to summon a farty wind spirit? What in the demon's sprinkle is this?" He tossed the book back on the shelf and wiped his hands down his pants.

"Oh! I know that one. Accidentally did it myself once. The summoning, not the—never mind." I looked away and quickly caught up with Fritzi.

The wooden floor gave way to a thin layer of carpet, swirled with odd symbols in a whirling, whimsical design. At the back of the shop were piles of newspapers, books, and articles, strewn atop a massive wooden table.

"Oh, look! It's me!" Fritzi said, picking up a news article and holding it in front of our faces.

I nodded, distracted by the mirror hanging crooked on the back wall. The antique wallpaper around it peeled, revealing black speckles of mold underneath. I inched toward my fairy reflection.

"Did you find something?" Henry asked, following my gaze.

"I think so. This mirror … it looks familiar. Almost like the one I have at home, except this one isn't enchanted. At least, I don't think it is." I stuck out my hand and traced the golden molded edges on the mirror. The hair on the back of my neck rose. I quickly glanced around the room to see if the feeling of being watched was only my imagination or if something more lurked in the shadows.

"Enchanted? You have an enchanted mirror? Let me guess. It can show you your heart's desire." He stood beside me, wiggling his brows, sticking out his tongue, and admiring his reflection.

"No. My mirror's more of an asshole. But I still miss him." I turned back toward the mirror and smudged my fingertip across the glass, but the mirror made no objections.

Henry nodded and made his way to a cushioned reading chair in the corner. The seat sagged under the weight of tattered magazines. He shuffled the papers aside, tossing them on the floor and muffling a faint sound of footsteps.

I cocked my head to the side to listen. The gait was swift, light, and agile.

"Vail?" I sucked in my breath.

"Look at this. It was lying right here, open to this page," Fritzi said, holding up a book with vampires drawn across the page.

I swallowed hard and shook my head at the dark figure standing behind her reflection in the mirror.

"No!" I screamed, whirling on my heels and barreling toward Fritzi.

The Council member lunged at her, but she threw the book in his face, causing him to stumble back. He bared his fangs and hissed in her direction. Henry rushed by us in a flash and slammed into the vampire, knocking him on the ground.

"No! Henry!" Fritzi screamed.

"Not in my store, you sick fuck!" came a deep, rumbling

voice I'd never heard before. The man's commanding tone vibrated off the walls, toppling over a few bookshelves.

An old man with wiry white hair stepped into view and pointed his gnarled cane at Henry and the vampire. A bolt of blue light shot out of the end, separating the two. As swiftly as he'd appeared, the old man brandished a stake from behind his back and muttered a word I'd never heard before. The stake flew toward the vampire, burying through his ribs with a sickening crackle of bones.

The old man rushed to the vampire's side and leaned down, pushing the stake further into his chest. "Tell me why. Why have you been sniffing around here? You're supposed to stay on your side."

The vampire's eyes met mine. He held my gaze until the last of his body quickly disappeared into a pile of ash. The stake fell to the ground in a loud thump.

"I take it, you two know each other?" The man stood up and brushed the ash off his knees.

"No. But I'm the reason he's here. I'm sorry I brought him to you." I inched closer to Fritzi, who stood, visibly shaken.

"Penelope, don't." Henry put his hand up, stopping me from saying anything further.

"She's a princess. You can't fool me, genie," the old man said. "I'm Abe. And I know everything. Don't act so shocked. I'm older than the entire Council. Do you think I didn't realize who you were? You smell of genie. Kind of like patchouli and molded incense with a touch of neediness."

Henry's jaw dropped.

Fritzi pulled a chair from the table and collapsed in it, rubbing her hands over her face. "I can't do this. We need to figure this out. What if Elly had been with us?" She looked at Henry and me and back again.

"Perhaps I can help if you tell me what the problem is and

why it's shown up at my doorstep, dressed as a fairy." Abe rested his palms on the end of his cane.

"I thought you knew everything already!" Henry threw his hands in the air. "Remember? I smell like neediness and mold?"

"That's true. But I don't know why vampires are suddenly coming to the city. He was the second one to come into my shop. One had arrived the other night and rummaged through these articles." Abe lifted his chin toward the table. "And this one, I imagine, hid in the basement until you three arrived. You're obviously what he was hunting for."

"I'm afraid you already know too much, sir. These vampires destroyed my home and my family. I've lost my powers from a curse, The Council wants me dead, and now, I'm stuck in this city without any spells or weapons or anything to protect me—us." I wrung my hands.

"A princess without her powers? Nonsense. You've traveled between worlds. You've got human blood in you then. Only creatures with human blood can do that. You're not a full-blooded princess." The wizard took a step closer to me, studying my profile.

"That can't be. I'm born of the sunflower. I'm my own DNA. I share it with no one else. I'm just cursed." My voice shook.

"I don't think you're cursed, dear. I think, somehow, you're mixed. Answer me this: have you ever found yourself performing dark magic? Witchcraft? Or as kids these days call it, bitchcraft?" His eyes bore into me as if he could reach into my thoughts with his gaze and read my truth.

"Yes," I said.

"Princesses don't have dark power in them. It's impossible. You're not cursed. You're part witch. Did you do something to piss off the vampires? They mostly hate witches, you know." He walked toward a bookshelf, leaning on his cane with each step.

"I'm not a witch. I can't do magic anymore. Look, I just want to go home. I don't want Fritzi and her family in any danger." I turned my face away from Henry and Fritzi, who sat, huddled in each other's arms at the table.

"Nonsense. You just can't do the magic you used to anymore. Doesn't mean you can't do any magic. Here, take these." He pulled books from the shelves and began to stack them on the table. "Go home. Read. Your answer will be in here. There are centuries of knowledge between these pages. And it doesn't take a wizard like me to sense the evil running through my community lately. I've tried to keep the peace between the worlds and offer this safe space for those who straddle realms. But there's too much darkness in both worlds; mixing the two is beyond what either world can handle. You need to go back to where you came from."

"What do you mean, mixing? You don't want to link the worlds?" I asked, wondering how far Finn had gotten on Priscilla's funded project to bring humans and the fantastical together.

"Heavens no! Why would I ever want them linking? That's a recipe for disaster! And not just for helpless humans, but for spell casters alike. Best not to meddle in that sorcery. You'll have the wrath of centuries-old wizards at your doorstep." His voice cracked like thunder.

"Oh. I never thought about the chaos it would unleash. I just thought …" I stammered. I had to run from vampires. I didn't want to run from wizards too. I had to warn Priscilla.

I picked up the books, piling them in my arms, but Abe kept adding more to the stack and mumbling. Henry got up to help me, but Fritzi remained slumped in her chair.

Abe paused, turning back toward me. "I won't ask you why you're so important to them. But I will tell you this. I saw the look in that vampire's eyes. He was hungry—and not for anyone or anything. He was hungry for *you*. Fritzi only got in the way. Whatever you did to them, they won't easily forget it. They're not going to let you go. They'll get you one way or another. In your realm or mine."

A ripple of fear crept up my spine. My life was doomed, no matter which world I chose.

CHAPTER FOUR

VAIL

I barely slept when Mirror Mirror woke me from my drowsy state. I rolled over, catching the scent of Penelope still lingering on her pillow. It was all I had left of her.

"Wake up, Vail! We got her! Look! Quick!" Mirror Mirror shouted.

I untangled my legs from the bedsheets and scrambled over to where he hung on the wall.

"That's a fairy! A big one too. Why did you wake me up for her?" I peered into the mirror.

"Nope. That's Penelope. I don't know why she's wearing a crazy outfit. Maybe for a disguise. But you can tell it's her. She's got the posture of a bow-legged moose. Look closer."

I rubbed my eyes and checked again. The fairy paused, staring directly at the mirror. She hurried over, inching closer, and peered back at me. There was no mistaking the soft edges of her lips or her jewel-like eyes tucked behind a row of thick lashes. A lock of hair, the color of honey, escaped from beneath her green wig.

I gripped the sides of Mirror Mirror and shouted, "Penelope! Penelope! Can you hear me?" My voice shook as I pleaded for any ounce of recognition I could get.

Penelope ran her finger across the mirror. A man stood beside her, making flirty faces at his reflection and chatting.

"She can't hear you. And we can't hear them. All we can do is watch and try to figure out where she's going or who she's with," Mirror Mirror said.

"He looks harmless at least," I said, watching them talk.

The man left from my view, but Penelope remained focused directly on me. I tore my gaze from the princess and watched the woman busily shuffling papers in the background. A few feet from her stood a vampire with The Council emblem sewn across his uniform.

"Oh no!" Mirror Mirror rattled against the wall. "Where did he come from?"

And that was when I felt her heartbeat pulsing through my veins in a vicious cycle. My adrenaline spiked.

"Penelope!" I shouted into a void, baring my fangs. But I was powerless.

The vampire lunged at the woman. Penelope ran to help, but the man from earlier rushed past her and tackled the vampire to the ground. I growled, grabbing Mirror Mirror in a tight grip. The princess's blood coursed through my veins at an alarming rate, giving rise to a wave of panic for us both. With each rapid pulse of her heart, I felt a knife-like ache in my chest.

"Fuck!" I yelled, curling my fists until my nails cut across my palms.

Drake burst through my bedroom door, splintering it in two and tearing my attention away from the fight in Mirror Mirror.

"What's going on?" He hissed through his fangs. His shoulders were perched tight around his ears, making him look bigger than he was—a trick he'd learned from the were-wolves, no doubt. He'd hated them only months ago, but these days, they ran in the same circles.

"It's Penelope! She's here. Wherever this is. I need to get there." I stared back at the chaos unfolding at the bookstore, but the vampire blew away in a cloud of hot ash. An old, hunchbacked man stood over the fading vampire.

"That's Penelope? She's at Abe's Emporium?" He rushed to my side and peeked in the mirror.

"I think she's in disguise. But she's probably there for a reason. She doesn't like to venture into the human world often. That vampire knew she would show up there," I said. I felt her pulse slowing and the heaviness of her guilt as she looked at the woman and man.

"He's a dumb vampire to even attempt anything at old man Abe's shop. That wizard could take on ten of us at once. If not more. She's safer there than anywhere else in Forks. Why's she in Forks anyway?" He scratched his head.

"Forks! That's where this place is! What's Forks?" Mirror Mirror asked.

"It's a city and a pretty big one. Couple of hours' drive to there from Morningwood. I've hunted there a few times for Priscilla. Maybe a little for myself," he said, looking away.

"Take me there," I spoke into Mirror Mirror, unable to tear my gaze from Penelope, who stood with the wizard.

"You mean, tonight?" Drake's voice lifted.

"Yes. Meet me downstairs as soon as the sun sets. I'll grab Ian. I can't waste any more time trying to defeat my enemy. I have to save my lover. It looks like they know how important she is to me now."

I watched as Penelope left the scene with the man and the woman. The wizard swept his palm over the vampire's ashes, vanishing them into thin air. I backed away from the mirror as the bookshop faded from my view.

"I'll be there. It's been a while since I've had some fun in Forks." Drake's mouth twitched.

"We're not going for fun. It's business," I said in a firm and final tone.

The young vampire's fresh appetite posed a problem I couldn't manage at this time.

"What do you mean, business? She's just your girlfriend. And why does The Council want Penelope anyway?"

I turned on my heels and grabbed him by the shoulders. He tensed, slinking back from me.

"Look at me. Are you part of this Bostwick brotherhood or not?" I glared into his empty eyes, searching for any hint of malice or treason.

He straightened his spine and stood upright, inches from my face. "I'm a part of this family. I know I'm the newest member, and I've not had the most stable history. But my loyalty remains with my brothers and with my commander, Leo's, cause. If you're questioning my motives, all I can give you is my word. It isn't worth much, but you'll have to trust me. It seems to me like you don't." He brushed a hair from his face and stared back at me.

Leo had once told me that Drake was a lost soldier without a war. He'd said he needed direction, command, and something or someone to fight for to get through to him. I never understood why Leo had taken the risk when he turned the young con man into one of us. But his skillset outweighed his questionable morals, and I trusted Leo's judgment of character enough to be honest with my brother.

"Penelope's the cure," I muttered, letting my hands fall to my sides.

"The cure? As in she'll give us our lives back?" He brushed his fingertips across his chest, lingering between his rib cage.

I nodded and crawled back into my bed.

"But how? Why? What?" Drake bounced on his heels.

His boyish enthusiasm became too much for me to handle. The violent scene I'd just witnessed had exhausted me enough already.

I waved him away. "We'll speak more about it later. Keep your mouth shut until then. Get some sleep. We ride at dusk."

He nodded, stepping over the broken door, and disappeared.

Grump let out a loud, gurgling snore on the rug beside me. I'd completely forgotten about the goat. He'd slept through the entire meltdown. I knew if he had been awake, he would have scored it a ten out of ten. I yawned, stretching my arms over my head.

"Look who's here to finally join us," Mirror Mirror said.

Trevor and Otto skipped across the floor in light, almost-inaudible steps. The fox and gargoyle team was as agile and nimble as vampires.

"Come on then." I patted the bed beside me, where Penelope had let them sleep.

They hopped onto the mattress and lay down, folding across one another. The soft sounds coming from the fox soothed me and gave me the comfort I'd grown used to when Penelope was around. Except she wasn't here anymore. She lived on the other side of a realm I hated visiting. The human world was too busy, too stiff, and too dangerous, especially for a princess. Penelope had to come home, and only I could get her here.

I rolled on my side and drew my knees up to my chest, curling myself under the blanket and burying my face into Penelope's pillow. I took a deep breath, silently thanking the vampire gods who had let us keep the gift of breath even if it was only a habit and an otherwise useless ability. Her scent filled my lungs, causing an ache to ripple through my chest. I slid my eyes shut and continued to breathe, losing myself in the memories of her until I drifted off to sleep.

I WRAPPED a heavy wool coat around me and shoved my arms through the sleeves. Drake had parked in the bustling parking lot of a nearby college bar. He'd said the bar stayed open until dawn, and we could easily blend in with the locals. But after pushing my way through crowds of twenty-some-things, I questioned my brother's judgment.

"I'm not sure why you think this place will give us any clues as to her whereabouts. We'd have been better off going straight to Abe's bookstore and asking the man himself." I raised my voice above the crowd as Ian and I followed Drake toward the back of the bar.

"You'll see," Drake said, casting a glance over his shoulder. "Besides, you saw what Abe did to that, uh, you know. He'd do it to us in a heartbeat too. I doubt he'll ever let a *brother* inside the shop again."

A thin, bony man stumbled backward into our path, knocking Ian over on a young woman sitting at the bar. Her cocktail spilled down the front of her sheer white blouse, soaking her chest with rose-hued liquid the color of diluted blood. Drake and I circled Ian in an instant.

"Hey!" She reached for a napkin and pressed it to the hollow of her neck. A small purple vein pulsed near the edge of her collarbone.

My fangs strained against the caps I was using to cover them.

"I'm so sorry, miss!" Ian said.

He reached behind us and snatched the man by the collar, shoving him in front of the woman. The man took one look at Ian and slumped forward. His long arms hung limp, dangling at his sides, as if he'd already given up the fight.

"Apologize to the lady," Ian said in a low drawl before he loosened his grip.

The woman slowed her hand and began to rub her fingertips lightly along her collar, dropping the napkin to her lap. Her eyes never left Ian.

"What's your problem, man?" the man asked with a squeak. He tilted his beak-like nose up, avoiding Ian's gaze.

"I said, apologize," Ian repeated, peering down at the man.

The woman straightened in her seat, tilted her head toward Ian, and parted her lips with a soft exhale. He raked his eyes from her mouth to the stiff, peaked nipples poking from underneath her wet blouse.

"Sorry. Jeez! I didn't mean to get in your way and push you into this lady's drink. I'm sorry, lady!" The skeletal man threw his hands in the air.

"Now, get outta here and watch where you're fucking going!" Ian shoved the man away.

He skittered away on spindly legs.

"Thanks," the woman said. Her chest rose and fell with each timid breath.

Ian licked his lips and tipped his cowboy hat at the lady before motioning for us to continue toward wherever Drake was taking us.

Drake twisted his mouth in a grin and led the way.

"We got time if you want to grab her and take her in one of the stalls," Drake offered as we neared an alcove at the back of the bar.

Two nondescript doors—one marked with *Men* and the other with *Women*—sat side by side, nestled into the black brick wall.

"We're here to work," I reminded him, rubbing my palm across my aching mouth. The thought of blood and lust pushed my fangs further down into their tight caps.

Ian threw his shoulders back and rolled his neck, stretching his spine to his full height. He adjusted his belt buckle and stiffened as a group of young women emerged from the women's restroom. They rushed by us in a fit of tipsy giggles and a cloud of intoxicating, youthful—fresh —blood.

"I'll be honest, boys. I'm fighting it," Ian said before running his tongue along the bottom of his caps. His eyes stayed fixated on the women's hips as they swayed out of view.

"We're all fighting it." I lowered my voice and took a deep breath, fighting off the temptation myself.

The more time we spent near humans, the blurrier the line between our instincts and moral code became. That was why, during Drake's work for us, Leo hadn't been as hard on him if he gave in to feeding or fucking. He was the only one of us who had to venture into the purely human dimension to do his work.

"Come in here," Drake said, pushing the restroom door open with his shoulder. He walked down four stalls, kicking open every door until he reached the last one. A handwritten note taped to the outside of the door read, *Out of Order*. "No one's in here, so let's do this quick."

"Do what?" I asked, watching Drake climb over the broken stall and drop down on the other side.

"Go talk with the people who can help us. If you can call them that," he called from behind the stall.

Ian jumped, grabbing the ledge of the stall and easily pulling himself up and over.

"What does that mean? Where are you taking us?" I asked, following them over the broken stall. "We're supposed to be looking for Penelope."

"And in a few minutes, you'll find her. Trust me," he said, searching my eyes. "I know I'm the new one here. But don't discredit my short time as a vampire for reckless stupidity. Remember what I used to do before this? I was in the under-ground scene long before I even knew vampires and werewolves and all that shit existed. Where we're going has nothing to do with our realm or this one. But if you want to find your princess in this big-ass city, you'll need some tools."

I nodded, biting back my skepticism.

Drake traced a series of symbols drawn on the side of the stall. A red laser-etched doorway appeared on the back wall and slid aside for us to pass.

"Listen up before we make our way inside. We're only there to see Herman. Do not, under any circumstances, speak with Phyllis. Do not even look at Phyllis."

"Who the fuck is Herman, and what's his problem with Phyllis?" Ian looped his thumbs under his belt buckle and chewed his lip.

"Why don't you just come out and say where we are?" I growled. My patience with my young brother was growing thinner by the minute.

"Because you'll scoff." Drake swiveled on his heels and headed down a dark hallway.

Red lights flashed along the ceiling, illuminating walls painted with graffiti, much like the restroom stall we'd exited. I hurried behind Drake, passing by a giant-sized, spray-painted blue dick, drawn with bulging veins and ball stubble. Ian grunted, clicking his boots behind me.

"I'm already scoffing. Wherever the fuck we are and whoever the hell Herman is, he'd better give us some answers. I'm losing my patience, Drake. Who knows where Penelope is by now?" I said.

We stopped in front of a windowless metal door. A glowing blue light escaped from the bottom. Drake put his palm to a sensor on the side of the wall, and the door opened.

"Brothers, welcome to a spaced-out speakeasy. Our alien overlords will be more than glad to meet you. They're very curious about the fantastical."

"Ah hell." Ian blew out a breath.

The metal door vacuum-sealed behind us.

Smooth jazz played over speakers as we made our way through the cylinder-shaped hall and into an open room awash in neon purple and pink lighting. The walls were lined with floor-to-ceiling windows looking out over a star-filled sky. On the far side of the room, a window reflected a purplish smoky planet.

"Smell that, boys?" Drake sniffed the air.

"No." I jumped out of the way of a robot barreling through the crowd with a tray of drinks.

"Exactly! There're no scents here—and no air. They don't need it. Lucky for us, we can't breathe. And lucky for them, we can't smell any temptation."

"Fuck. Very lucky indeed," Ian muttered as a gorgeous creature with skin the color of the ocean's edge sashayed right past us in a sheer white skirt that barely hid whatever the hell was tucked underneath.

She wore a gold pastie over each of her six breasts, lining her chest in two rows. A metallic tattoo flashed from beneath her dusky skin. She turned her head toward Ian and winked.

"That's what I call a six-pack."

I tore my eyes from her and scanned the room. I'd seen aliens before at The Cave. Bruno regularly brought in tentacled creatures for live shows. But I'd never been in a room full of extraterrestrial beings, especially one resembling a dimension I never cared to visit.

"Are we still on Earth?" I asked Drake.

"Yep. It's just designed to look like we aren't. Pretty damn impressive, isn't it? Bet you didn't know I could sneak us into a place like this." The corner of Drake's mouth lifted into a smirk.

"I'm impressed. I'll be even more impressed when you tell me how this is supposed to help Penelope."

"Then, right this way." Drake held his palm up, sweeping it across the room.

We walked past a crowded bar. The ten-armed robot behind the counter had his metal hands in bottles and glasses.

"That's our wine!" Ian pointed out as the robot poured from a bottle of Bostwick Black Label.

"Yep. It's popular. I've sold them eighteen cases this season. They're one of the biggest supporters of our cause without knowing it!" Drake wound his way through the mixture of weird and weirder.

Something that resembled a giant fried chicken leg with one eye sat, playing on a grand piano tucked into the back of the room.

I dragged my feet after Drake, scanning the room for signs of my princess or anyone who looked remotely normal enough to help us. But between the foxtailed women parading around in nothing but stickers and the ten-foot-tall blue men with long, flowing antennas, I wasn't hopeful.

"Herman! It's so good to see you. Please, meet my brothers Vail and Ian. They're the faces behind Bostwick Black Label. Brothers, this is Herman," Drake said as we approached a corner table with a circular booth.

I bowed at a two-headed creature with snouts like alligators. The bigger head had eyes like a snake, but the smaller head had googly eyes. Legit rolling-around, googly eyes with big-ass pupils.

"And Phyllis!" the small head shouted. Her eyes shot in opposite directions.

I immediately averted my gaze, paying Phyllis no attention, as per Drake's orders. I had no choice but to trust my brother in a place like this. I'd never seen anything like it.

"Ah! The famous Bostwick brothers. You're quite the celebrities. It's not often we get to see those from the other,

other dimension. Have a seat! What brings you here? I know if Drake's here, there's bound to be a catch. I'm guessing someone needs murdered." Herman's voice came out deep and low like a croak. He slithered sideways, making room at his booth for us to sit.

"Murdered," Phyllis hissed. Her eyes rolled back, blinking at the back of the booth.

"No, not at all." Drake made the first move to scoot in next to Herman, followed by Ian and me.

A robot wheeled itself in front of us, placed a bottle of Project X on the table, and began to pour us each a glass.

Herman took a sip of the smoking cocktail in front of him and peered over the rim.

"You want information then," he said, leaning forward on the fattest elbows I'd ever seen. They resembled two loaves of bread, doughy and crusty all the same.

"Yes." Drake took a long sip of his wine and licked his lips, sighing. "They save these few bottles special for me. It's the elf batch." He popped the caps off of his fangs and stuffed them into his front pocket, smirking before leaning back into the booth.

I ignored my brother and pressed on with the conversation. "Drake said you might be able to help us find ... my girlfriend. She's not from this world. She's from ours. But her abilities are broken, and now, she's here. The problem is, we don't know how to find her. We've no idea where she went. Can you help?"

"Can I help?" Herman laughed.

"Ha-ha-ha-ha!" Phyllis threw her snout back and laughed loud enough to draw the robot bartender's attention.

His metal eyelids flipped up and down in one big blink.

I looked to Ian for help, but his attention remained focused on the flirty six-breasted alien from earlier. She sat at a table in the back corner, surrounded by similar-looking creatures.

"Herman knows all and sees all. And he doesn't need magic to do it. He's head of security in Forks. He has cameras stationed on every inch of the city. Every street, every tree-top, every forest, every park, every car, and every house. Course, the humans have no clue. These aren't their precious government cameras. Herman's are the size of a pinprick." Drake took another long sip of the bloody wine.

Herman reached under the table and grabbed a handful of tiny specks of glitter from his pants pocket—or whatever he wore down below. Fear and disgust kept me from peeking under the table to see what the bottom half of this creature looked like. He tossed the glitter in the air with a dramatic *ta-da*. It floated down onto the table, attaching across the top.

"All cameras," he boasted. "That's my magic."

"Wow! They're so tiny! What do you use all this technology for?" I rubbed my hand across the glittery table, but the cameras stuck onto the top like glue.

"Information and resources. And I'm afraid that's all you're getting out of me. But I do owe this brother of yours a favor. So, I'll help you with your girlfriend."

"Who's got a girlfriend? Herman, you cheatin' bastard!" Phyllis snapped her jaw in the air. Her two oversize front teeth hung low in her mouth.

I scratched my head, avoiding Phyllis's googly eyes.

"We last saw her at Abe's Book Emporium. It was earlier today, probably around lunchtime. We need to know who she was with and get their address, so we know where she's at," Drake said.

Herman swept his hand across the table, clearing the cameras and turning the tabletop into a screen. He typed across an invisible keyboard, and the screen faded into a map. His fingers flew across the map, pushing buttons here and there until he paused the camera feed right as Penelope and the man and woman stood outside of Abe's.

"There she is." I let out a breath.

"Damn," Ian drawled.

"I'm not finding any information on her. But the man and woman she's with live at 22 Blasko Street. That's outside of the city. They go by the name of Cox."

"Cox!" Phyllis squawked before roaring with laughter.

"Fritzi Cox! What in the world is your girlfriend doing with her?" Herman's mouth hung open, displaying rows of teeth sharper than my fangs.

"I don't know. Who is she?" I asked.

"She's a journalist and a novelist. We read her articles. It's one of our only links to your world. In case, you know, we need to harvest your resources one day too." Herman cleared his throat and sat up, looking for a challenge.

"Oh," I said, not buying into this prodding.

"I always knew Fritzi had connections, and here's my proof that she speaks the truth!" Herman swept his hands back over the table. The camera feed disappeared.

"Thanks. We'll be on our way then." I began to scoot over on Ian, pushing him out of the booth.

"You won't make it by dawn." Herman tilted his head toward a giant window in. The sun edged around the corner.

"Dun-dun-dun!" Phyllis sang.

"Think there are any rooms for rent upstairs?" Drake sat up, looking toward a long staircase, which disappeared into another level on the opposite side of the room.

"It's been a quiet night. I'm sure they do." Herman drummed his talons across the table, and Phyllis bobbed her head.

"Thank you, Herman. I appreciate your help. Next batch of Black Label is on me." I slid across the booth and stood up before making my way toward the stairs.

Ian tipped his hat and followed behind me.

Drake snatched his glass of wine from the table and caught up to us. "Wait! Let me check us in. They know me. They don't let any vamps in here. That front door only opens for me and maybe, like, five others."

"I feel like this is a dream. I have no clue what just happened." Ian rubbed his face.

"Me neither. But at least we have an address." I rubbed my temples and drew a long breath.

The six-breasted alien brushed past us, trailing her sharp fingernails across Ian's back. She wiggled her hips up the staircase and paused, casting a glance over her shoulder.

"Hey, uh, you think I can get my own room?" Ian tugged at his collar.

"Dude, you ever tried to drink an alien? They're cold-blooded, like us. I don't recommend it." Drake shook his head and winced.

"I didn't say I wanted to drink her. I've got … other needs right now. I'm not hungry. In the world of humans, we're just animals. Right?" Ian's eyes followed the alien as she made her way up the stairs.

"Go on. But as soon as the sun goes back down, we have to get to Penelope. Especially before The Council does." I stepped aside, letting Ian pass.

He took the stairs two at a time, hurrying to catch up to the seductive creature.

"Man, he's in for a wild night." Drake continued up the staircase and checked us in at a desk in the loft.

The receptionist was another six-breasted alien and just as flirty as Ian's woman.

"Drake, dahling. The usual?" she asked, stroking her collar with her fingertip.

"Ah, no. I've got my brothers with me tonight. Only a

room to get a quick break and hide from the sun, please." He ran a hand through his hair.

I stood back, watching their exchange and picking up on the other six-breasted aliens coming and going from the numbered rooms.

"Room fifteen." She handed Drake a card.

"Thanks, Tilly." He dipped his head and made his way past the desk and down a hall.

"Drake?" I said, shuffling after him.

"Yeah?"

"I'm impressed. I had no idea you were this involved in things."

"You never asked." He stopped in front of our room and pressed the card to the reader on the wall.

"I'm sorry." I swallowed hard.

We stepped into the room. Drake flipped a switch on the wall, and pulsing rainbow-colored lights turned on underneath the beds. The real reason for the rooms upstairs suddenly clicked in my mind. We were in a space brothel.

"I know I can do dumb shit sometimes. And my youth makes me a target for temptation. But I'm a Bostwick, and I take my fight for the cause seriously. I hope you can see that now." Drake pulled his shoes off and tossed them aside.

"I do see it." I kicked my shoes off and shuffled to one of the double beds before falling back down on it and staring at myself on the mirrored ceiling. "You'll need to bring Finn here sometime. To the bar, not the brothel. He'd love all the technology. If you can drag him out of his damn lab. He'll go mad, staying in there much longer. But he's devoted to the cause too." I sighed. "The things we do for life."

"And the things we do for women." Drake plopped himself on the other bed. "We'll get her back tomorrow. Though after that, I don't know how ..."

"I know. Me neither. I just want her safe in my arms. The rest I'll figure out later."

"Aye, aye, boss."

The walls rattled in a rhythmic thump. Moans carried over from the room next to us.

I bit my lip, stifling a laugh as Ian's voice yelled, "Giddy up." The sharp smack of flesh against flesh cracked loudly.

"I'm going to pretend this isn't awkward as fuck and go to sleep now." I cringed.

"Yep. Nothing to hear or see. Night!" Drake put a pillow over his head and quit moving.

I fluttered my eyes shut and fantasized about Penelope and the way her skin prickled under my touch. With each moan from next door, my cock thickened. A fire of desire spread throughout my body as I replayed our lovemaking in my head.

My mind jumped to the last night we'd been in bed together, giving each other oral sex. Her blood soared through my veins while she worked the crown of my cock with her tongue. She was reckless and wild in her desires, urging me to bite her harder. I took two long gulps of her blood from the inside of her thigh as she hovered atop me, still wrapping her lips around my dick and sucking. Blood had trickled down her leg and onto my cheek before I cried out for release and spilled into her warm mouth.

I needed my princess now.

An ache of grief punched me in the gut as I curled up beneath the blanket and forced myself to sleep. The sounds of pleasure next door lulled me into a jealous and miserable slumber.

CHAPTER FIVE

PENELOPE

I SHUFFLED MY FEET DOWNSTAIRS, FOLLOWING MY NOSE TO THE scent of magic bean water. A half-empty mug sat on the table amid a stack of books.

"Morning, sunshine!" Henry appeared from around the corner and handed me a cup.

Sunshine.

The word punched me in the gut. I hadn't been called that since the compliment slipped from between Vail's lips.

"Thanks." I took the mug and filled it to the brim.

"Have you looked outside yet?" He pulled open the freezer and rummaged through the cold stash of food before pulling out a bucket and opening the lid.

"No. Is someone out there?" I cupped my coffee in my palms and made my way to the window.

"Not someone. Something. Something exciting! And fluffy!"

"A bunny!" I nearly spilled my coffee. My love of woodland creatures still simmered beneath my surface.

"Nope! Better!"

I peered out the kitchen window and into a glistening winter wonderland. Fluffy, giant snowflakes whirled through the air, silencing the outside world in the muffled hum of the season's first snow.

"Look! It's snow!" Fritzi rushed past me with Elly on her hip, sliding across the kitchen in her worn house slippers. She pointed out the window and grinned. Both girls were still bundled in pajamas and bathrobes.

"Sssssnoo," Elly babbled, her tiny lips curling into an *O*.

I'd never experienced winter outside of Poppycock, much less with humans. But when Fritzi had come downstairs with Elly and shown her wide-eyed daughter her first snow, I became enchanted too.

"Oh my gosh! That's the cutest thing I've ever heard. Can she touch it?" I set my mug down and bounced on my heels.

There was something magical about snow, even in the land of humans. The look of awe on Elly's face was catching. All four of us shared her curious expression.

"I think she'd love to touch it. Want to show her?" Fritzi stretched her arms out, offering Elly to me.

"I, um … I …" I said.

"Go on. Take her, Auntie Penelope. I'll get her hat and coat and you one too!" Henry said, disappearing from the kitchen. He came back in an instant, tossing me a coat and helping Fritzi wiggle Elly into hers.

I pushed my arms through the sleeves of an old, fluffy coat and wrapped it around me before sliding on a pair of shoes.

"Here," Fritzi insisted, pushing Elly into my arms.

Elly looked up into my eyes and cooed, and it hit me.

Baby. Fucking. Fever.

I melted.

"Hi!" I said, staring down into her big blue eyes.

She grinned and hid her face in my shoulder.

"Aw! She's shy!" Fritzi kissed the top of Elly's head before wrestling her noggin into a knitted hat.

Elly thrashed her head back and forth and pulled the hat off.

"No, no, silly! You have to wear the hat to see the snow!" Fritzi put the hat back on her daughter.

Ssssnoo, Elly mouthed.

"Yes! The big white stuff outside. Auntie Penelope is going to take you to feel it."

"Nel Pee?" Elly pointed at my chin and bounced in my arms.

I curled my arms around her tighter.

"Yes, that's Auntie Nel Pee!" Henry said between mouthfuls of something that looked vaguely like snow.

"Really, Henry? Ice cream at this hour?" Fritzi shook her head and made herself a cup of coffee.

"With sprinkles! Can't go wrong with rainbow sprinkles. Here, try." Henry opened a drawer and took out a spoon. He scooped the ice cream and opened his mouth, nodding at me to do the same.

I drew my brows together and opened my mouth, letting him feed me as if I were his daughter.

"Hey, that's pretty good. Kind of what I would think snow tastes like." I swallowed the cold cream and headed toward the door before Elly could object.

Anything her dad ate, she had to have it too. Just last night, Henry had introduced me to hot sauce. He put it on everything—beef, eggs, pizza, and veggies. He even thumped the bottle over a potato chip and gave it to Elly to quit her whining. It didn't. The little girl still asked for more.

"Let's go, Elly, before your dad turns me into a cow," I said, unlocking the back door and stepping outside.

"Moo," Elly whispered.

My ovaries twitched—again. If babies could remain this cute forever, I'd need to get myself one of these things.

"Hold out your hand," I said, balancing her on my hip and taking her hand between my fingers. I stretched her arm out wide and tried to catch a snowflake.

We hopped along the backyard, my feet crunching into the snow until a snowflake landed right smack dab in the middle of her tiny palm. She curled her fist around it and laughed. But when she opened her fingers again, it was gone. She stuck her trembling bottom lip out and looked up at me.

"It melted. It's gone," I said in a sad voice. "But it's okay. There's more! Want to catch another?"

I didn't wait for her to answer before I took off dancing with one hand on her and the other stretching her little chubby hand to the sky. We whirled with the snowflakes, weaving in and out of the gusts of wind.

Elly's cheeks reddened from laughter and the chill in the air.

"Bibbidi-bobbidi a la ka zoom!" I laughed, moving Elly in between my palms and zooming her through the air.

We spun up a cloud of sparkling white flakes. They twisted and turned and flew through the air, soaring above us and forming into a flock of doves.

I gasped, pointing up at the birds as they swooped down, circling us with the loud hum of their wings. I pulled Elly tighter to my chest and cradled her head, placing my palm over her ear. We stood still in the middle of the whirlwind of birds until shouts from Fritzi and Henry broke the spell and scared the doves away. They flew off into the sky before disbanding into snowflakes and floating into the distance. On the ground, surrounding my feet, grew rows of deadly, spiked icicles standing four feet tall, boxing Elly and me inside their walls.

"What the fuck?" Henry shouted, running to grab a shovel

from the side of the house. He immediately began hacking away at the thick icicles.

I carefully handed Elly over the spikes and safely put her in her mom's arms.

"Still questioning your witch lineage?" Fritzi asked, clutching her baby to her chest. A brief hint of terror crossed her face.

"Yes. If I were a witch, I could straddle the realms and go back home. But I can't. I don't know what I am. I thought I couldn't do magic anymore. I have no idea what that was!" I stepped through the small gap Henry had cut through the icicle wall.

"I'll admit, that shit was wack!" Henry breathed heavily and tossed the shovel aside.

"Shit! Wack!" Elly repeated.

"No!" Fritzi cut her eyes to Henry.

"Sorry!" Henry held his hands up. "But it's true though."

"Nel Pee." Elly reached her hands out to me and made a grabbing motion with her fingers.

Fritzi drew her daughter closer to her. "I think it's time to go inside."

A pang of guilt washed over me. Whatever joy I'd felt in those first few moments in the snowfall had quickly fled away on the back of those doves' wings.

I SPENT the afternoon trudging through the snow and losing myself in the woods behind Fritzi's house. After my incident with Elly, I didn't want to stay close. To keep Fritzi and her family safe, I had to get away. I twirled and sang far away from their home, but no matter what I tried, I couldn't perform magic. I did my best to re-create what had happened with Elly to cause the ice spikes to form, but even with muttering the same song and skipping the same dance moves, nothing happened.

By the time the sun set, I gave up and resigned myself to searching the books I'd brought back from Abe's shop. But the mood in the Cox house grew silent and awkward. I knew as much as my friend wanted to help me, she wanted to protect her daughter more.

So, I made up my mind to leave first thing in the morning, no matter what. I was going back to Morningwood. I'd pick up the pieces of my burned cottage myself and live like an old hag in the woods, far away from Fritzi, Elly, Vail, and anyone else I might harm. At least until I could gather the strength and wisdom I needed to avenge my godmother and end The Council.

I flipped through the pages of a leather-bound grimoire dated back two centuries ago. The incantations scribbled down looked familiar. I recalled reading some of them in the books Gertie had asked I study when I practiced magic. But instead, I had wallowed in a pool of self-pity and wine.

"Are you two getting anywhere?" Henry asked, leaning on the office doorframe.

His eyes drooped under the weight of Elly's bedtime routine. The little girl had fought with every ounce of energy she had, battling against her own will for rest. Fritzi and I had listened through the thin walls as he sang her a nursery rhyme I'd never heard before until the sobs finally stopped.

Fritzi's fingers clacked across the typewriter in a steady rhythm.

"If you're asking me, this article won't write itself. I've got about two more pages to type before I can focus on anything other than my job. But if you're asking the princess over there with her feet up, maybe," Fritzi said. She kept her eyes on the paper in front of her.

"Who? Me?" I questioned Henry, twisting my body around on the worn couch before sitting up.

He settled in a nearby armchair and hooked his feet around the chair legs before folding his arms behind his head and sighing. He raised his brows and nodded toward the stack of books beside me.

"As a matter of fact, I did find something useful. These spells here are labeled bitchcraft. Priscilla, the witch in Morningwood Manor, mentioned bitchcraft to me before. She thought I had it in me. And that makes sense if I'm to listen to Abe too. He also said I was part witch. So, if I'm a witch, I should still be able to practice magic, right? It's just different here."

"How can a princess be a witch? I thought you were born with new blood and not DNA from someone else?" Fritzi stopped typing and took a sip from the coffee mug beside her. Similar cups, all empty and sticky with old magic-bean residue from days before, littered her desk.

"That's what I don't know. But if I'm a witch, I need to find out." I tossed the grimoire aside and picked up a tattered, old history book stuffed with articles.

"Hmm." Henry leaned forward and tapped his chin. "If you're a witch, then you'll be able to cast spells with witchy stuff here. I think that's how it works. Salt, candles, a rat tail. Witchy shit."

I pulled out articles from the book and spread them on the coffee table.

"Here, you look through these and see if you can find a list for witchy shit. Maybe we can pick some items up tomorrow, and I'll test myself." I shoved a stack of papers toward Henry.

He shuffled them into a pile and set them on his lap before leaning back into the cushioned chair.

I rifled through more articles, sweeping them aside until I

came across a faded report from a historic news journal, *Starlight Press*. I picked up the paper and stared at a picture of my godmother and Priscilla on the front.

"It's Gertie," I whispered, squinting my eyes and bringing the paper closer for inspection.

It was dated nearly a century ago.

"No way. Your godmother?" Fritzi stood up and hurried over to the couch, settling in beside me.

"Yeah. That's her all right. And Priscilla. She's the one funding the Bostwick labs." I brushed my thumb across the page and read the article aloud.

TWO YOUNG WITCHES MAKE HISTORY IN THEIR ENCHANTED GARDEN

Gertie Fern and Priscilla Ankerton aren't your typical witches. This best-friend duo has taken the witching world by storm with their antiaging breakthroughs.

"It really only started with beauty and skin care," Priscilla said. "But after we noticed a spike in energy and health, we began testing for longevity."

The two witches met at a local garden nursery and quickly connected over their passion for science and beauty. When Priscilla's husband, Loure Ankerton, a successful business owner, suggested they make their own oils and tinctures, the unstoppable pair jumped on the idea.

"It was really Loure who started it all. He gave us the idea and invested in the business," Gertie said. "And the rest is history. Priscilla and I immediately went to work, brainstorming different products to stock at our future apothecary."

However, their quest to cure crow's-feet recently took a different turn when a cursed herbal potion they'd created extended the life expectancy of a butterfly by two weeks, doubling its life span. The witches re-created the brew and continued testing. All of the butter-

flies lived longer than initially predicted. After a year of successful attempts, the witches knew they were onto something.

"We had no idea our tinkering would eventually lead to scientific breakthroughs. We wanted to turn back the clock on aging, as in wrinkle prevention, not extending life," Gertie claimed. "This breakthrough opens a world of possibilities."

But when asked about their secrets to turning back the clock, Priscilla cut the interview short. "All I can say is, our methods aren't conventional or easily replicated. It's going to take a lot of work on our end, but you can expect more things to come from us, and hopefully, that will include a longer life."

"Holy broomsticks!" I set the article back down on the table.

"What's it mean?" Fritzi picked up the paper and examined it.

"I have no clue! But Gertie never told me they ran a business together. I can totally see Priscilla being into antiaging but not my godmother. Or the life-expectancy thing. That's dark magic! I think. Isn't it?"

"It is," Henry said, reaching for a nearby spool of bubble wrap and crushing the bubbles between his thumb and forefinger—a move Fritzi had said he made when he was nervous. Henry pushed himself off the chair and paced the room, popping the bubble wrap as he walked. His light-up shoes sparked with each step. "Stopping death or bringing back someone from the dead or even delaying death—it's all dark. Genies can't even dabble with it."

"Was Gertie a dark witch? I didn't even know she was a witch. I thought she was a godmother." Fritzi pinched the bridge of her nose. "I can't keep anything straight."

"Godmothers can be anything, but they're mostly witches. You have to apply and go through a rigorous process. There's no way she was a dark witch. The Princess Oversight Committee would never allow anyone with dark magic near our patches. I wonder why she never told me any of this. I didn't even know they were once that close. When she told me they were old friends, I thought it meant they maybe bunked together at school—not that they had created time and extended life. Damn. Their falling-out must have been serious."

"Didn't you tell me you were living in Priscilla's cottage and she was supposed to help you with your magic? Maybe she owed your godmother a favor." Henry paused, flinging the bubble wrap aside and picking up the article and studying it.

"Maybe. She's also the one funding the vampire research. Which, now, I get. I bet she's having Finn work on extending life along with working on the vampire cure."

"It was probably a deal. He does that for her, and she funds the research for him." He set the article back down.

"I need to get to Bostwick and speak with Finn. He has to have more information."

"But why? What good would it do? How would it help get you back?"

"I don't know. But he can communicate with Priscilla. I can't. She's full-blooded and unable to travel here. I can't see her."

"Hold on!" Fritzi jumped to her feet and rushed over to her typewriter. "I can communicate through words."

"Yes, darling. You're the best at it. But this isn't the time to pat yourself on the back." Henry stood behind her, stroking her hair. She swatted his hand away.

"Not that! I mean, I can write something we can get back to Priscilla or Vail or anyone on the other side. Since words are the only link we have. That article you read from, it's not from this world, obviously! Unless it was written as satire for a Halloween press or something. And it clearly wasn't. So, let's write. What shall we say? And to who?"

"To Vail." I swallowed hard. I knew my vampire lover was on the prowl for me, and if I stayed here much longer, he'd find me. And who knew how many of The Council was trailing both of us? I had to lead him back home. He was safer with his brothers. "Just write, *One, two, three. One, two, three, three.*"

"Huh? *One, two, three. One, two, three, three?*" Fritzi asked.

"Yes. He'll know where I'm going." I picked up the article again. A chill crept up my spine as I stared at the picture of Priscilla and my godmother. I ran my fingertip along the edge of the paper, setting it aflame. I jumped, fanning the article and extinguishing the fire.

"How'd you do that?" Henry gasped.

"I don't know," I answered.

A loud knock thumped against the front door, startling all three of us.

"Who could it be at this hour?" Fritzi glanced at her watch and pushed herself from under her desk.

A tingling sensation vibrated through my fingertips, and a spark of light flew from the tip of my thumb. The hair on the back of my neck rose, standing on end.

"I don't think you should answer it," I said, shoving my hands under my arms.

Henry drew himself up to his full height and flared his nostrils. For a brief moment, I caught a flash in his eyes.

"You two stay. I'll get it." He crept out of the office and down the stairs.

Fritzi walked out into the hall, guarding the door to Elly's room. I followed behind her, pausing at the top of the stairs to listen.

We waited until Henry came back.

"There wasn't anyone there." He shook his head.

But the feeling of dread remained, vibrating deep within my bones and bursting forth to get out.

"Or someone we can't see. Someone not from here." Fritzi placed her hand on the doorknob to Elly's room.

"We need to go. I'm going back to Morningwood, and you three are going to find a place to stay for a while. I'll send word when I've handled things and it's safe to return." My fingers twitched as I struggled to hold back whatever was happening to me.

"But what about—" Henry started.

The putrid smell of something rotting filled the air.

"I said, we need to go now." My voice came out deep, raw, and nearly demonic—the same as it had when I was at The Cave with Priscilla.

FROM THE DESK OF FRITZI COX

Dear Reader,

In full disclosure, I've been documenting this story as it happens or as it's been recounted to me. But this is the point where Penelope's story ends. I've decided to set aside my typewriter and move my family to a safer location for the time being. The chapters following this are pure speculation. Until Penelope finds me again, I can't guarantee the truth in what comes next.

By the time I left Penelope back in Morningwood, something had begun to transform inside her and was slowly working its way out. Not long ago, the princess I'd picked up from jail was frightened, skittish, and most of all, lost. But the woman I dropped off today was anything but confused. Penelope kept her chin up and didn't even shed a tearful good-bye. Her distracted mind was noticeably elsewhere. Her entire persona had changed, and oddly enough, even her hair had grown with streaks of an almost-purplish, inky-black hue.

She waved me good-bye with an air of confidence. Whatever my friend had set out to accomplish, I had no doubts she'd get there. The spark in her eye reminded me of my husband's from long ago when he'd lived as a genie with a purpose. She might no longer be a princess, but she no longer needed to be one. Her transformation during the short trip back to her home was incredible, and I knew Gertie would have been proud of her goddaughter's newfound independence.

As per the princess's request, I'd left a note at my door, directing Vail to the location she'd told me about earlier —*One, two, three. One, two, three, three.* But I worried my friend's bravery was also borderline stupidity. She wasn't thinking clearly, and I couldn't blame her grieving mind. So, before we'd left, I'd attached the article about Penelope's godmother and Priscilla with my letter to Vail in hopes that they would reunite, and if she caught herself in a bind, he would know to look to Priscilla for answers.

As for my family and me, we are hunkered down and safely hiding with friends with no plans of returning to our home until our courageous heroine finds us again or sends word that it's safe. But rest assured, as a dutiful reporter, I will keep you up-to-date with the latest and continue my research for truth and transparency.

CHAPTER SIX

VAIL

"Faster," I urged Drake.

"I'm going as fast as I can. These police officers aren't werewolves! We don't want to get pulled over around here. We're out of our element. Besides, we probably look suspicious enough, driving around the suburbs at two a.m." Drake checked his rearview mirror before pressing further down on the gas pedal.

"We get there, and then what? The Council is probably watching the place." Drake said.

"Good. Let The Council show up while I'm there," Ian snarled from the backseat.

"No. We don't want them anywhere near Penelope or her friends. If she trusts them to keep her safe, they're good people. I don't want to mix humans with the shit we were dealt in life. We're trying to cure our evil ways for a reason." I rolled down the window and let a burst of cold air hit me in the face.

A pair of bright lights rushed toward us, sending a faint

thump of a heartbeat racing through my chest. Drake swerved the car, narrowly missing another vehicle barreling past us.

"Fucking human drivers!" he yelled.

Ian glanced behind us, reading the bumper sticker next to the car's taillight aloud, "*Baby on board.*"

"She's close. I felt a heartbeat." I clutched my chest.

"It's because we're in her neighborhood." Drake turned down a street lined with cookie-cutter homes and manicured lawns.

"Can I feel?" Ian asked, scooting closer to the front, reaching for my chest.

"It's gone. It was only a flutter." I drew my brows together.

Drake pulled into a driveway. All of the lights in the house were off.

"I don't think they're here," Drake said.

"It's late. They're probably sleeping." Ian sat back in his seat and opened the door.

I swung my legs out of the car and took a deep breath before quietly shutting my car door. I could already smell Penelope's intoxicating scent. She smelled of sunshine on crisp cotton sheets left on a line to dry or sunflowers in a field refreshed from rain. But it was her taste that drove me wild. She tasted like summer, all bright days and sultry nights.

"No, Drake's right. At least, I hope he is." I bared my fangs as I nudged the side door. Someone had left it cracked open. "Come on," I whispered, entering the house.

My senses were on high alert. I became aware of every sound, every step, and every movement in the home. A fan whirred from a room down the hall, the refrigerator buzzed in a low hum, and from upstairs, the soft chimes of a music box played. Drake and Ian followed behind me in silence, nimble on their toes yet poised to attack. My eyes easily adjusted to my dark surroundings—another perk of my disease.

"Someone's here, and it's not the princess," Ian said.

"They're upstairs. Where the music's coming from," Drake answered.

"Shh. Stay behind me. I'll go first." I inched down the hall and past a dim night-light until I stood at the bottom of a carpeted staircase. I reached out, grabbing the railing, and swiftly pulled my hand back. My palm was glazed slick with a goo I'd never seen before. I brought my fingers closer to my face, inspecting them for blood, but found nothing, except slime.

"Jeez. What the hell is that?" Drake took a step down, away from me.

"I don't know, but anything this disgusting can't be good." I swallowed hard and pushed myself forward, eager to find answers to my princess's whereabouts.

The music grew louder. I couldn't rest, I couldn't think, and I certainly couldn't move on without Penelope. She'd found her way into my thoughts, my senses, and into whatever was left inside my chest. She was my heart.

We reached the top of the stairs and passed by an office, scattered with cups and papers. An overturned mug lay in the middle of a puddle of coffee on an unraveling and aged rug. Piles of books were stacked atop a table, littered with plastic wrappers and empty bowls. The wall thumped, knocking down a framed portrait of the couple I'd previously seen reflected in Mirror Mirror.

My brothers and I hissed, showing our fangs to whatever lurked in the dark. I motioned for them to go to the room next to us, where the soft music played. A putrid smell wafted around the corner, sending all three of us into a gagging fit. I burst through the door of the room and clenched my fists.

"Hey! What're you doing? I was about to drop some sick beats!" A grotesque goblin sat in the corner of the room, surrounded by oversize stuffed animals. He scratched his butt.

A mobile hanging over a crib spun in the soft melody we'd heard from downstairs.

"A fucking goblin! You have got to be kidding me." Ian marched toward the crib and pulled down a pink quilt, exposing an empty bed.

"I'm not just any goblin! I'm Big Glug-Glug. You heard?" The goblin folded his chubby arms across his naked chest.

"Ah, yeah! I've seen you at The Cave!" Drake stepped into the room and picked up a stray sock, examining it.

"See? I'm famous. Now, let me work." Big Glug-Glug reached for a rattle beside him and held it to his mouth, vibrating breaths from between his lips in a catchy rhythm.

I tore my attention from him and searched for signs of the baby—or worse, what was left of her. Toys lay strewn about the floor, and drawers hung halfway opened, spilling over with clothes. The scent of baby powder and milk lingered faintly under Big Glug-Glug's sickening breath.

"Why are you here? And where's the child? Did you see a princess?" I walked to the crib and ran my fingertips over the soft mattress, picking up the warmth it still held.

Big Glug-Glug stopped rapping and stared at me. "I'm here for Henry, of course. He was supposed to help me get a gold chain. But I ate his ex-girlfriend, who just so happened to be this kid's grandma, and then he died. And, well, it's a long story. Not really, but I'm too lazy to tell it."

Ian flew to his side in an instant. "Tell it."

"Sheesh. Yo, I didn't hurt anyone. I was going to ask if he'd get me a gold chain. That's all. But he couldn't even see me, and neither could anyone else here. I hopped through the front door, right under his feet, and besides a crinkle of his nose, he didn't notice me. Guess he's full human now. I'll never get a pimp chain." He raised the rattle in his hand and opened his palm, letting it fall to the floor like a mic drop.

"None of that matters. Was there a woman with them? Blonde, bubbly, rosy cheeks, and eyes like jewels?"

Big Glug-Glug put his fist to his mouth and stifled a laugh. "My man's whooped!"

Ian gave the goblin a hard nudge with the tip of his boot. "Answer him."

"All right, cowboy! Damn. Yes, she was here. She is fine too. If I were Henry, I'd be back in my big blue dildo and coaxing them both up on deez nuts," he said, grabbing an area that was thankfully hidden below a giant fat roll.

"I'm going to ignore whatever the hell you meant. Just tell us where they went and if they're safe," I said.

"How should I know if they're safe? They seemed spooked to me. And it wasn't because I was here. They ran around, throwing stuff in suitcases, and Fritzi left this by the door. I can't read, but maybe it'll help you." He lifted his leg and pulled a damp envelope from underneath him. "As I said, I was only here for my chain. I didn't hurt anybody. Henry's my boy. What'd you think, I eat babies or something? You're the evil vampire. I'm just a chubby toad of a monster." He handed me the envelope.

"Watch it," Ian said, kicking Big Glug-Glug again.

The goblin fell over, leaving a trail of goo.

"I don't think he means any harm," Drake said, hoisting Big Glug-Glug back up.

"Thank you, fan. I'll send you an autograph." Big Glug-Glug brushed off his shoulder and leaned back on a giant stuffed teddy bear.

I tore open the letter and started reading it.

Dear Vail,

I have your princess, and she's doing well. She wanted me to tell you, "One, two, three. One, two, three, three," and leave it at that. I'm assuming it's an address or code word. So, I'm doing my duty and reporting it back to you.

However, I feel something isn't right. Since yesterday, Penelope has been acting even more peculiar than usual. It seems she's not able to perform her princess spells, but she's still capable of something. I saw it myself this morning when she danced with my daughter in the snowfall.

Something changed in Penelope after that event. The grief and sorrow she'd displayed when she first arrived melted away as fast as the snow. I've no time to explain more. Just know that she's been safe, and I'm taking her to wherever she tells me to back in Morningwood. I have to cut this short, as after we found the article, things turned rather strange quickly, and we have to go into hiding.

Please see the attached article, as it might help you in saving her. Penelope didn't want me to let you know of this. I think she's trying to protect you. But I don't want to see my friend hurt, and I have a feeling she's about to be in a lot of trouble.

I've done all I can. We won't return here until it's safe, so please don't send anyone looking for more information.

I'm sorry I can't help you further. I have a child, and I can't put our lives at risk. I wish you the best.

Fritzi

I pulled the yellowed article from the envelope and skimmed it. My eyes immediately fell on Priscilla's name.

"It's Priscilla. We have to go to Morningwood Manor." I stuffed the papers back into the envelope.

"What?" Drake held his hand out. "Let me read it."

I handed it to him and let him read it aloud.

"What's, 'One, two, three. One, two, three, three'?" Big Glug-Glug tapped a stubby finger on his third chin.

"It's our dance moves. She's telling me to go to the ballroom. But she won't be there. She's leading me away. She's at Priscilla's." I turned on my heels and flew down the stairs.

My brothers chased after me.

"You don't think Priscilla has anything to do with this, do you?" Drake yelled from behind me. His voice held an edge of panic.

"Only one way to find out," Ian replied, hopping down the stairs three at a time.

Big Glug-Glug cleared his throat and loudly began rapping about fangs and bangs as we rushed out the door.

"At least we gave the fat bastard new material," I muttered.

"Fuck this human-world shit. This trip couldn't get much weirder. Fucking aliens and celebrity goblins. I'm ready to go back to Morningwood. I can't handle much more drama." Ian tipped his hat and shook his head.

"But first, to the witch's lair." I opened the car door and slid inside before slamming it shut.

During our entire drive home, Drake didn't speak a word.

WE ARRIVED BACK in Morningwood right before dawn. The winding roads led us straight to our town, tucked away on the edge of a small range of mountains. The horizon lightened in a splash of pinks and corals, peeking up over the hills that hid the entrance to our city.

"We'll not make it to the manor. We have to get back to the winery now. You can't save Penelope if you're a pile of ash, and I, for one, don't want to burn up," Drake spoke for the first time since we left Fritzi's house.

I blew out a breath, knowing he was right.

"If we had Project X, we could replenish our energy. But

that doesn't help our sun allergy." Ian rubbed his hands over his tired eyes.

"Look, we won't get far unless we rest and eat. There's no way we would be a match against Priscilla or whoever unless we're at our best. We don't have a choice," Drake said.

"Head to the winery. We'll gather ourselves and make a plan after we feed. I'll have Finn supply us with human blood, so we're at full strength. But I'm not leaving Penelope in harm's way. We need to send her help." I drummed my fingers across the dashboard.

"We don't even know if she needs help. I've worked with Priscilla for a while now. Just because some old article related her with Penelope's godmother doesn't mean a damn thing." Drake swerved the car, turning down the road leading to Bostwick.

"I'm not saying she has anything to do with this. But I am saying, she has to know something. And we know Penelope is there. You really think she went back to the ballroom, where she'd witnessed a massacre?" I said.

"Or back to her cottage …" Drake's voice trailed off.

"No. I doubt she'll ever go back there. You didn't see the look in her eyes when she faded. There's nothing left for her there. She probably doesn't want to remember that night."

"But Leo would have wanted us to—" Drake started.

"Leo's not here!" I raised my voice. "He's gone. He isn't coming back. We're all in this together. I'm sorry if you feel Priscilla betrayed you somehow or if you're having second thoughts about working with her. Did you not know she was evil? She kills virgins, for crying out loud. You've helped her with it! I don't judge, and I haven't asked questions. But how can you not have a bad feeling about this?"

Drake flinched. "I'm not having second thoughts. I'm only saying, we shouldn't jump to conclusions. No one knows what's happening."

"I think she does," Ian spoke up. "That lady has always rubbed me the wrong way."

"Look, at this point, we have no choice but to march in there and demand answers. All signs point to Priscilla. And if that's the first place I suspect Penelope will go—and it is— I'm there. I need Penelope and not only because she's our chance at life. I need her because I love her."

A weighted hush seeped through the car until Drake broke the silence. "You feel it? The raw emotions and feelings? How's that possible without mortality? We're dead inside."

"Maybe not all of us. I don't know. I'm sure drinking the blood of a sunflower princess has something to do with the taste of life teasing me. But who knows? I love her, and I don't care about the why or how. I do care about the *if*. If I don't tell her and she leaves this world, not knowing, after she has no one left? Heartless or not, I'll feel pain." I rested my head against the cool glass window and stared at the passing fields and vineyards as we loomed closer to home.

"Have you told her you love her?" Ian asked.

"No. I didn't even know it until she left—cliché how that works. You know the old saying, *You don't know what you've got until it's gone*? Well, she's gone. And it fucking sucks." I sighed.

"But how do you know it's love? It could just be some fling." Drake white-knuckled the steering wheel as he rounded the corner to our driveway.

"Some fling." I blew out a soft breath between my lips. "I'd happily take a stake through the chest if it meant Penelope would one day flash her dazzling smile again. She could watch me pass and dance in my ashes, and as long as she danced, I'd feel like my job was done."

Drake's eyes darted to Ian's in the rearview mirror.

"I know what you're thinking. I'm working for the cause

—don't get me wrong—but I'm also working for love. And lucky for me, Penelope's both," I assured my brothers.

"Then, let's save your princess." Ian took off his cowboy hat and held it to his empty chest.

A dreamy, far-off look clouded his gaze, and I knew a memory of his wife was crossing his mind.

CHAPTER SEVEN

PENELOPE

I walked to Morningwood Manor from a wooded area where Fritzi had left me. She'd been reluctant to leave me in the forest, but I'd told her I had to stop by my old home to make sure I hadn't left anything behind, and then I'd return to Vail's. But my lie couldn't have been further from the truth. I wasn't ready to go back to my cottage. The memories were too raw for me to think about, much less experience all over again.

I needed to get to Priscilla, and even though I couldn't see her in this realm, she was powerful enough to figure out a way to communicate with me. Ever since I'd read the article about her and my godmother, I knew there was more to my story. I felt different, as if reading the words had sparked something new and darker inside of me.

My heart fluttered, but if I came close enough for Vail to feel my pulse, he couldn't get to me anyway. The sun shone overhead, blazing down on my scalp. I raked a hand through my hair, twirling a tendril of black locks around my finger.

Whatever was happening to me wasn't just a phase. The set of my jaw, the length of my spine, the clench of my fists all propelled me forward into whatever dark secrets awaited me.

I grabbed the door handle and twisted my palm around the once-enchanted knob. But there wasn't a hint of charm in the rusted copper. When my godmother had brought me to visit Priscilla, Gertie had had a long conversation with the charming fellow. But now, he was nothing to me, and I was nothing to him. We existed on separate planes.

"Hello?" I called, pushing the door open and stepping inside.

The door slammed shut behind me, knocking a puff of dust from a nearby candelabra.

"Priscilla?" I tiptoed inside the entry and stared down the long, dark corridor lined with flickering gaslit sconces on either side of the arched stone.

"Priscilla, I know I can't see you anymore. You're just a ghost to me. But can you let me know you're here? I have a few questions. It's about Gertie."

A warning whispered in my head. The voice sounded familiar and laced with an edge of terror.

Godmother?

I swatted away something crawling on the back of my neck. A spider hung from its web, dangling from my fingertip.

"Ugh!" I dusted my hand on the leggings I'd borrowed from Fritzi. She'd told me no one wears dresses anymore. With leggings, I'd get more agility, and I could roundhouse-kick anyone in my path. Whatever that meant. I hadn't had the energy to ask.

"I'm going to take a look around then, I guess." I began making my way down the hall.

A forceful gale rushed toward me, knocking me back

onto the rocky floor. I landed on my bottom in a pool of something cold and wet.

"What the hell?" I brought my palm to my face and flinched.

Thick, bubbly blood covered my hands and back. I scrambled to my feet and reached for the door, but it quickly locked.

Laughter rumbled down the hall, vibrating the glass panes in the windows until a few of them shattered. I shielded my face from the window closest to me and began to shake as my imagination took the best of me.

"I'm going now!" I yelled, backing myself into a wall.

But the long, brittle silence that followed told me otherwise.

I shook the door handle again.

Locked.

A sickening groan echoed down the hall. Footsteps slowly dragged across the stone but got louder as it came near. My mind floundered. I shut my eyes tight and hummed, trying to recall any spell I could to get me out of here. The footsteps stopped. I opened my eyes but still saw nothing. I hummed again, but the footsteps picked up their pace.

"Go away!" I yelled into the dark abyss. A cold knot formed in my stomach. "I said, leave me alone!"

A heavy stone smashed against my skull from behind, knocking me to the ground. I heaved, on my knees, racking my lungs to catch my breath. But the blows kept coming and showed no signs of relenting. I rolled out of the way and turned around, facing my attacker.

Screams built at the back of my throat as I stared into a man with no face at all. He had no eyes, no nose, no mouth. His skin was pulled taut over his head, as if it had been sewn after someone harvested his parts.

"You're her zombie. I met you. Get away from me!" I kicked at the zombie.

He caught my foot and pulled me to him. My back scraped against the cobblestone as I fought him off. My vision blurred from the blood dripping into my eyes. I swayed on my bottom, nearly losing consciousness. My eyes fluttered as I struggled to catch my breath.

"Please. Please let me go," I muttered.

But the zombie only grunted. His emotionless groans chilled me to the bone. He walked around to my back and grabbed me by the hair, winding it around his fist. Searing pain rippled along my spine as he dragged me down the corridor by my hair, kicking and screaming. My skin tore beneath tattered clothes.

I reached behind me and clenched his foot, cracking his brittle bones with my hand. His foot fell right off.

"You like that, asshole? Huh?" I screamed, jumping to my feet, still holding his foot.

He fell to the ground in silence, impaled by my stare.

"That's right, bitch! This little piggy is mine, motherfuck-er!" I held his foot in the air, shaking it around. Bits of skin and bone fell to the floor.

A howl of wind came from a nearby hall. I turned my head to look in the direction of the noise, but before I could react, an entire army of spiders marched toward my zombie attacker, swarming his motionless body and dissolving him into a pile of skin and goo.

I held my sides and bent over, gagging and gasping for air. The putrid smell of rotten flesh overtook me as I fell to my knees. I brushed a spider off my ankle and cried. Icy fingers curled around my neck, invisible to my eye. But the long fingernails digging into my collar didn't fool me. Priscilla wouldn't let me go.

"It's you. Traitor!" I screamed, clutching my neck. But it was useless.

Her grip closed around my throat until I could no longer speak. My breath caught in my lungs as I struggled for air before my world went black.

I WOKE up on the cold stone floor of a cage. The metal bars instantly reminded me of my short stint in the jail cell as soon as I'd left Morningwood the first time. I'd fought my way out of that predicament with help. But here, I had no one.

"Priscilla! What the fuck?" I screamed. "What do you want from me?"

No answer.

I gripped the iron bars and shook. The cage didn't move. I could barely see anything in the dimly lit room besides a small desk in the corner, littered with papers and candles, which had burned into a puddle of wax.

My teeth chattered as a draft blew in from somewhere that I couldn't see. I dropped to my bottom and hugged my knees, trying to warm myself. The air hung thick, suffocating me into gasping, shallowing breaths. My throat ached, slowly swelling and closing up. I squeezed my knees tighter, rocking back and forth, silent and defeated. I'd stupidly walked into this trap, and now, I was paying the price.

I swallowed hard, biting back tears. All the time I'd spent planning vengeance against a douche-bag ex-fiancé, I could have spent bettering myself and learning my truth. I would have had to figure it out at some point, and Gertie would have been forced to explain. But instead, my mind was preoccupied with people who didn't deserve my time. Even dancing with Vail was an act of retribution instead of an act of love. Sure, I'd fallen for him after we spent a substantial amount of time together. But I couldn't see what was right in front of my face while it happened, just like I couldn't see Priscilla for the treacherous bitch she was.

A heaviness settled in my chest. I let my eyes roam the room for any possible means of escape, so I could warn Vail and the brotherhood about the witch. But nothing could save me now. I brought my palm to my neck and rubbed the tender parts. The sudden realization that Vail could be dead overtook me, turning my stomach and building a sour taste at the back of my throat.

"Priscilla!" I screamed. My voice came out ragged and raw. "Priscilla, please! Can we talk? Get a pen and parchment or something! Communicate with me. I know you can figure it out!"

For a moment, I thought about asking her to send Drake, but I didn't want any of Vail's brothers around this psycho bitch.

I pushed myself to a standing position and called out again. This time, she answered. The candles on her desk lit themselves one by one.

"How come you can see me, but I can't see you?" I asked faintly as the clicking of heels loomed closer to me.

The air grew frigid. I stuck my face between the bars and blew out a breath, sending a cloud of vapor in front of me. Priscilla's face emerged in the fog, inches away. She shot me a twisted smile. I screamed and fell backward, panting in terror.

From somewhere down the hall, a grandfather clock chimed nine times. I could only imagine what nightfall would bring in a haunted mansion.

"Fa-la-la-la," I tried.

But my princess magic failed. I could no longer summon

a swarm of butterflies, let alone anything capable of mauling my captor to death. I was doomed.

A burst of high-pitched laughter echoed off the walls.

A flash of outrage coursed through me. "Better watch out! Remember that bitchcraft? I can still do it!" I warned an invisible foe.

The blaze on the candlesticks burned brighter as the footsteps trailed off in the distance. A rush of wind blew a stack of papers from the desk. The old parchment pieces twisted in a whirlwind before slipping through the cage and falling at my feet.

I blinked, staring down at article after article. I scooped a few in my hands and began to skim them for any clues as to what the hell was going on and why I sat, locked away in my godmother's friend's mansion. I read articles on Priscilla and Gertie's advancements. They'd created a line of vitamins that renewed skin cells at an alarming rate, a line of makeup that camouflaged the wearer to blend in with her surroundings, and a shampoo for hair growth.

"What's this have to do with me?" I tossed the papers in the air and kicked the pile of articles in front of me.

Underneath my shoe was an article from the same news journal, *Starlight Press*, that had printed the first article I'd read about my godmother and her friend.

DREAMS, CREAMS, AND SCREAMS: HOW THESE
ENTREPRENEURS WENT UP IN SMOKE

Gertie Fern and Priscilla Ankerton were taking the world by storm until their business and dreams went up in flames. This incredible duo's line of age-renewal products had become one of the best-selling skin-care lines our world had ever seen. Infused with enchanted and charmed DNA, their top product—a facial moistur-

izer—had won multiple international awards for combining technology, magic, and natural ingredients.

But the cream had its drawbacks. The highly flammable material used as one of the over two hundred ingredients in the moisturizer would self-destruct after it hit expiration. The witch team had altered the product to vanish the day of expiration, but a batch of cream kept in storage slipped under the radar and ruined their entire business.

Gertie came in early to check inventory and found the warehouse up in flames, and no amount of magic could extinguish it.

"I tried every spell imaginable. The fire in those pots roared with life. That was what we were creating—longevity. But we suffered the consequences after one small compound was left unchecked. The lasting ingredients fueled the fire, so to speak," Gertie said.

The entire apothecary's warehouse, which also harbored their greenhouse, turned to ash in the wee hours of yesterday morning.

"Our products were destroyed. Everything was destroyed. And then it all vanished," Gertie said.

When asked what the future held for their business, Priscilla declined to comment.

I unclasped my fingers from the article and let it drift to the floor. It disappeared before my eyes, fading away in a puff of smoke.

"You cursed me. To vanish. You think Gertie had a part in the fire, so you cursed me to get back at her." I stumbled back to the far side of the cage.

The candles atop the desk flickered. My head swirled with doubt. Godmother would never destroy anything unless she had good reason. I dropped back down to my knees as the steel weight of misery closed in on me.

"It's done and over with. You win. You cursed me and killed my godmother. You might as well end me now. I have nothing left." I stiffened, preparing myself for whatever blows were coming my way.

But the sound of slamming doors and harsh voices carried from outside the room. Priscilla's candles blew out. A low rumbling shook the walls, rattling the rafters hanging from the ceiling. A sprinkling of dust swirled down into the cage.

My heartbeat hammered against my rib cage. The voices drew nearer. I caught a hint of a low country drawl in a shout.

Ian? Ian!

I opened my mouth to scream, but something hot lashed across my face, splitting across my brow. I wiped the back of my hand across my forehead and examined it. My blood shimmered in the dim light, coating my knuckles in a thick, sticky streak the color of garnet. I winced, rocking back on my bottom, and passed out.

CHAPTER EIGHT

VAIL

The closer to Morningwood Manor I came, the quicker Penelope's blood—what was left of it—pulsed in my veins. With every thump of her heart, I felt a jolt in my chest.

"Penelope! Penelope!" I kicked the door open, ignoring the doorknob's screams. I didn't have time for charms.

"Maybe we should have snuck in. Who knows what lurks in here, Vail?" Ian grasped my elbow and stopped me.

"That's why I have to get to her now," I growled, jerking my arm back and staring down the dark hall.

Candles flickered on either side of the stone walls, barely illuminating the mossy cobblestone underfoot.

A large rat crossed our path before stopping at a puddle on the floor.

"What the fuck is that?" Drake said, inching closer.

"It's blood! Fuck! Fuck! Fuck! Fuck!" I ran my hands through my hair and picked up my pace.

The trail of blood dotted the floor before coursing down the hall in a river of red.

"Penelope!" I shouted.

A guttural sound came from around the corner.

Ian threw his arm out in front of me, preventing me from going farther.

The sound croaked again. I stuck my nose in the air and drew in a breath. A rotten scent blanketed the crossway, knocking us back against the wall.

"I'm going to check it out," Drake said.

"No. Let me." I shook my head.

"Relax. I can handle it. I'm here all the time. I know my way around here better than you do." He put his hand up, stopping me.

"Fine. But be quick. We need to keep moving." I tipped my chin in his direction.

He waved me away and hesitated before rounding the corner and stumbling back. He lost his footing, crashing into the floor. He skittered backward across the stone, scraping his palms along the moss and sliding his heels through the slick blood. He slipped onto his back with a thud.

I jumped from the wall, posed to attack. "What is it?" I asked, baring my fangs.

"Zombie. Even worse than usual. He's just … goo. Let's get out of here. Come on. I'll take you to Priscilla's study. She's probably there." Drake wiped his hands down his pants and stood up.

I nodded before motioning for Ian to follow. I inched my way into the darkness but stole a glance at the zombie as we passed.

"Jeez." I gagged, holding my arm to my nose.

A mess of decaying skin and rotten innards oozed, trailing rancid blood down the corridor.

I breathed a sigh of relief and continued the search for my princess. The sconces lining the long hall flickered, sputtering out one by one.

"Faster," I yelled to Drake up in front.

He picked up the pace and jogged toward a set of double doors.

"Ha-ha-ha-ha-ha!" A woman's cackle echoed off the bare walls.

"Fuck!" Ian slipped, falling to his knees.

I turned around and swiftly pulled him up by the elbow. He brushed the dirt off of him before running.

The laughter grew louder, deafening.

"Almost there!" Drake shouted.

The quicker we ran, the farther the double doors at the end of the hall grew. We ran past more hallways—some blinking with ghostly apparitions or crawling with rats while others disappeared into a dark void.

"We're never going to get there!" Ian shouted, running beside me.

"Just keep going. Don't look back and don't look into the halls! Focus on the doors." Drake flew across the floor ahead of us.

"Fat fucking chance of that. Did you see that kid back there? The one holding the doll? Fuck this shit!" Ian's voice shook.

I'd never seen that expression of terror in any of my brothers' eyes. But Ian looked ahead of him as if he were staring at death's door.

A fluttering startled inside my empty chest.

"We're close. She's here. I feel her." I quickly side-eyed Ian before returning my focus forward.

Ian slowed, pausing. He kneaded the back of his neck and drew his brows together. "Feel?"

I stopped running. "Yes. She can make you feel again. I didn't want to tell you and put you in danger. But we're here, and this doesn't look like it will be a walk in the park. What-ever it takes, we have to save Penelope. She's our cure."

"Feel," he muttered, rubbing his chest. His eyes snapped back to mine. "Giddy up. Let's lasso that asshole witch and get Penelope the fuck out of here." He pushed on his heels, barreling forward.

The hallway grew silent.

Drake waited at the doors. "You ready?" he said.

"Let's get our girl," I growled.

The door creaked open, revealing an empty, expansive room with curved walls and a smoldering fireplace. Dirt and rat shit littered the floor.

"What a good boy. You brought them right to me. Now, your brothers will no longer be a problem." Priscilla cackled as Drake rushed to her side. She stood up from behind a desk lined with a row of small skulls dripping with melted candle wax. Her lips parted in a sinister grin.

My fangs dripped with poison, numbing my tongue and stinging my lips.

"Delivered, as per your request." Drake bowed and avoided my gaze.

"Drake? You lied to me? You did this? I thought you were my brother." A pain shot through my chest, curling my toes. I stumbled back.

Ian hissed beside me.

A draft blew in from a broken window, stoking the flames in the fireplace.

"All isn't fair in love and war," Drake said, wrapping his arms around Priscilla's bony waist and kissing her on the mouth. Her slender fingers trailed down his back.

"You fucking asshole!" I ran toward him, but Priscilla stuck out her hand and sent me flying back with a forceful gust of wind.

"You won't get away with this," Ian shouted from beside me. His fangs hung low, peeking from beneath his upper lip.

"But I already have." Priscilla laughed. Her voice carried,

echoing back down the corridor. The walls groaned, as if in response.

"Where is she?" I asked, searching the room.

"Oh! This will be fun. Come, let me show you where your princess resides." Priscilla's black eyes sharpened as she swept her palm in our direction.

An army of spiders marched down the walls, falling down needlelike threads and crawling over toward both Ian and me.

I screamed, brushing them away but it was useless. They overtook me. Their spindly legs crawled up my shins and to my arms, where they went to work, bobbing and weaving. Before I could understand what was happening, they'd pinned my wrists behind my back in a thick web wrapping.

Ian shouted beside me, struggling against the critters. But they kept coming in droves, marching over us until they finished their job.

I shot a pleading look at Drake, but he refused to meet my gaze.

The spiders left as quickly as they had come.

I wrestled against the webs.

"There, there. Now, you won't try any funny business. Follow me." Priscilla's heels clicked against the stone floor as she led us back out into the corridor and down yet another hall.

I exchanged glances with Ian, who stood, staring at Drake's back. His wrists strained behind him, but the silk threading might as well have been made of iron.

"Chop-chop! You're straggling behind. I thought vampires were supposed to be speedy! Drake never has any issues with keeping up." She shot a smirk over her shoulder. Her jowl snapped loose, sagging before she shook her head and tightened it up.

"No virgin maidens to kill off in a while, eh? I guess

Drake isn't so speedy after all. You look like a fucking corpse," I spit out.

"Ha! Aren't you cute? I'll have my maiden when I drink from your precious princess." She threw her head back and laughed.

"She's not a virgin, dumbass!" I shouted, lunging forward.

Drake pushed me back.

"Pfft." She blew out a breath. "Course she's not. She'd put out for any prince who told her she was worth something. It turns out, she really is. Heh. Imagine that." Priscilla continued until she reached a splintered wooden door.

"Let's reunite these lovers, shall we?" She gave Drake a playful bop on the nose and opened the door.

I squinted, peering around the room. In the far corner, Penelope sat on the floor of an oversize birdcage. Her tattered sweater hung loose on her small frame. She had her bare feet tucked under her, hugging her knees to her chest.

"Don't mind that rusty, old thing. It's all I had. It was for my new dragon, but … Bruno couldn't secure that project for me. Good thing I found the perfect use for it though." She dangled a key in her palm before stepping aside and letting me through.

"Penelope!" I cried, rushing to her.

"Vail?" She jerked up to her feet, pushing her reddened cheeks against the iron bars. "Vail! I'm here! I'm here!" she shouted. A cry of relief broke from her lips.

"Penelope!" I ran to her side, straining my arms against the spiders' silk threads.

I wanted to touch her. I needed to feel her. I had to hold her. Her heart thundered in my chest, filling me with restless energy I hadn't known I carried.

"I'm so sorry. I'm so, so sorry," she stammered as I neared her. A deep gash creased her brow, splitting it in two.

I shook my head, stepped into her, and crushed my lips to

hers, muffling her cries. She opened her mouth and returned my urgency, thrusting her fingers through my thick hair. Tears flowed down her face, staining my lips with a salty sweetness. I pressed my cheeks into the metal bars of the cage, trying to get to her.

She pulled back and wiped an arm across her mouth, sniffling.

"You have to go," she whispered, reaching out and clutching my hand.

I stood back, noticing the dark streaks in her knotted hair and the blood caked around her collar.

"I'm not going anywhere. What's she done to you?" My eyes roamed her figure, checking for more damage.

"I'm fine. But you weren't supposed to come here. I was supposed to be back at the winery. I thought I would find out more information about my godmother. There's this article." She kept her voice low.

"I know. I read it."

"You what?"

"Enough of this opera." Priscilla sighed, dramatically wiping a fake tear from her cheek.

Penelope flinched, shrinking back in her cage.

"Vail, your princess can't see me or hear me. She's powerless here. It's because of my amazing, badass spells on the manor. It protects me. Anyhoo, I need one of you vampires to translate some things back to her. And if you're a good boy—like my lover, Drake—I'll spare you ... but you'll be far away from Morningwood. Got it?" Priscilla said with a smirk.

I turned away from Penelope.

"What's she saying?" Penelope asked, twisting her hands together.

"Tell her, Vail." Priscilla took a step closer to us. Her smile vanished.

Ian looked from me to Priscilla and hissed. She waved him away.

"She wants me to translate for her." I gritted my teeth. The pounding of Penelope's heartbeat ached in my chest.

"I don't understand how she can see me or hear me, but I can't see her!" Penelope threw her hands in the air and twirled, singing in a sinister voice I'd only heard once before —the night she'd cursed The Cave.

Priscilla laughed. "Your magic won't work here. You're in my territory now, and it's sacred ground. The portal to link the worlds is right here, and Drake and I are close to making it work both ways. You'll see me soon enough. But don't think your spells will work on me. I've years on you, kiddo. Centuries even."

I repeated the information back to Penelope.

Ian shifted on his feet, inching in between Priscilla and me.

"We can't let her do that." Penelope shook her head. "Vail, we have to stop her. It'll be a disaster!"

"I'm more concerned with you right now, Penelope," I said, clenching my jaw. "What do you want from her? Why is she here, Priscilla?"

"I need her blood." Priscilla folded her arms across her chest and drummed her fingers.

"Why? You're not a vampire, and she's not a virgin maiden. She's hardly of use to you. She doesn't even have any powers! She's a human! I'll get you whatever you need if you let her go."

"Ask her about Gertie, Vail," Penelope pleaded.

"Yes, about that old hag. You know what? This is nonsense!" She threw her hands in the air and chanted in an authoritative tone that turned my stomach. Her fingers flew out in front of her, pointing directly at Ian. She tilted slightly back on her heels and grinned.

The room filled with laughter.

Ian screamed, as if an invisible force had ripped him in two. His body convulsed, falling backward onto the ground. He shivered, writhing in pain until the room quieted. His eyes grew icy and unresponsive without any sign of life.

"That's better," Ian said, rocking back and forth on his bottom until he caught his footing and stood back up. His arms remained tied tight behind his back. "I could get used to this vampire body. It's so … what's the word? Empty." He shrugged his shoulders. "Now, where were we? Oh, yes, speaking of your meddling godmother." Ian glowered at Penelope.

Drake set his jaw and took a step away from Priscilla. Her eyes had turned completely white, rolling back into her head as she held her trance over Ian and possessed his body.

Penelope fidgeted on her feet. "Why didn't Gertie tell me much about you? Why did you give up on the apothecary? And why am I locked in a cage?"

"That's a lot of questions. You know I hate small talk, so I'll get right to the point. Your godmother is the reason you're here. Once upon a time, Gertie and I were best friends and business partners. We created things. Dark things. We were on the edge of creating longevity through seeds—princess seeds. Harvesting princesses would give us immortality. I wouldn't need virgin maidens anymore. Goddess knows they're hard to come by these days," Ian said in a long drawl.

"You wanted to grow princesses and kill them?" Penelope asked.

"Yes."

"Children?" Penelope asked.

"Easier when they're small."

Penelope fell to her knees.

I scrunched my nose and stared at Drake, twisting my

wrists against the webs holding me back. He still avoided my gaze. Instead, he focused on Priscilla—protecting his precious villain from his own brother. I cursed myself for ignoring the twinge of skepticism I'd had when it came to his trustworthiness.

"But Godmother would never do that." Penelope stifled a sob.

"No. She's too much of a Goody Two-shoes. So, she went one way, and I went the other. But not before she burned our laboratory to the ground. All of our work was lost. And I've been trying to get it back for ages. Although Finn has been useless in his endeavors. He couldn't re-create a gnat if it flew into his lab." Ian stole a glance at Drake, who nodded in agreement.

"Finn's helping you too?" I asked.

"Do you think I'm funding your silly cure for vampirism for you?" Ian laughed. "Hardly. I couldn't care less what you dumb vamps do. You'll never find the cure for your disease anyway. It's a waste. While Finn is harvesting DNA for you, he's also harvesting it for me. He has the underground greenhouse, where there are rows and rows of little seeds incubating. Though, as I said, no luck yet. He's useless. But my Drake here, he's got some tricks up his sleeve."

"None of this makes sense. If Gertie was afraid of you, why did she bring me to you for help?" Penelope stood back up, gripping the metal bars.

"I'm guessing she did it to trick me. She brought you here under the guise that you were troubled or cursed and nothing more. She took a risk, so I wouldn't be suspicious. And I'll admit, it worked. Until I saw you in The Cave. Princesses don't perform bitchcraft. Not even ... troubled ones," Ian snarled, looking down his nose.

"But apparently, I do," Penelope said, flicking her wrist and trying to cast another spell.

"How many times do I have to tell you, your magic doesn't work here? You're not even a princess. Well, not technically. Your godmother planted you. I suspect she'd stolen *my* seeds and kept meddling with our old longevity potions and spells long after she burned our apothecary down."

"But that's not possible. No one could have planted me. I just bloomed. Fate and shit."

"Nope. Not you. You're special—and you're mine. I'd created the formula to make you. I'm guessing she didn't realize how attached she would become to you if her little experiment worked. And it did because here you are. Unfortunately for her, her curse didn't help you at all. I'd ingrained protections in my seeds. The older you became, the darker your magic grew. I had known precious princesses like yourself would need all the protection you could get."

"What do you mean, my magic didn't fade? It only changed? Then, why did I disappear?"

"Your magic faded because she'd cursed you. She wanted to banish you from the magic realm to keep you safe. She cursed you with the same vanishing magic we'd used at the warehouse. It was her, not me. If anyone ever knew what you were, you'd be locked away in a cage and used for torturous experiments forever." Ian opened his mouth in a wide grin. "But before you faded, you changed. Your attitude, your spells, hell, even your hair."

"Godmother cursed me? I don't believe it. I lost my home, my fiancé, everything. She wouldn't have done that," Penelope spoke in a quiet voice.

Ian shook his head. "The lengths that woman went to protect you. Lie after lie after lie. She thought bringing you to Morningwood would keep you safe." He blew out a long breath. "The best lies are those right under our nose. Gertie thought I wouldn't catch on to you before she faded her precious abomination of a daughter. She knew, without her, you would disappear completely. But when your magic began changing instead of fading, she got scared. She needed you gone from this world. Otherwise, she knew you were destined to be found—by me. Her final act to save you was the fire."

Penelope shook her head, shuffling her feet backward until she reached the other side of her cage.

"No. It's not true. You killed her!" Penelope screamed, pointing at Ian.

"No. I would have eventually, but I only kill virgins and sweet little blooms. Your godmother killed herself. I always knew she was a lot more conniving than I gave her credit for. She must have really loved you to sacrifice herself to save you. Pity it was for nothing because you're mine now." Ian's evil laugh rang out through the room, bouncing off the walls and vibrating deep into my nerves. A satisfied light flashed in his eyes.

"You didn't send The Council to kill Gertie? And to kill Penelope?" I swallowed hard and stared at Priscilla and Drake, realizing Priscilla had no idea Penelope was our cure.

"Why would I do that? The Council came in only to kill Theo—you're welcome, by the way, Penelope—and to scare her a bit. I needed her on my team. I wanted her to feel like I could protect her, so she'd work with me and hunt down the rest of the cursed princesses out there. I know Gertie didn't just steal one seed. That old bitch was smarter than that."

"But The Council destroyed everything! They didn't only kill Prince Theo, Priscilla. They destroyed Leo and a whole lot of guests! Not to mention, our labs." I changed the topic away from Penelope.

"Oh, yes. Well, oops." Ian giggled.

My fangs dripped poison, causing my tongue to tingle.

The numbing effect traveled down my throat, slowing Penelope's pulse in my chest.

"What do you want from me?" Penelope asked. She slumped against the back of the cage and sighed.

Her heartbeat wasn't slowing because of my poison. She was giving up.

"Immortality," Ian answered.

"Penelope, look at me." I caught her gaze, holding it. I thumped my palm across my chest. "One, two, three. One, two, three, three," I whispered. "Don't give up now."

"How cute. You think you can dance your way out of this entanglement." Ian swayed his hips and laughed before his voice deepened in a vile tone. "Now, be a dear, Drake, and kill your brother. I want him to watch what happens when people meddle in my affairs."

"No! You said you would spare him," Penelope shouted.

"You still haven't learned, have you? I knew princesses were dense, but I had no idea you were downright dumb. Tsk, tsk. I lie. I'm evil. I kill anything that crosses my path. Do I have to do everything myself?" Ian huffed, shutting his eyes and muttering a series of chants. The webs circling his middle ripped apart.

"No!" Penelope screamed, tossing herself against the rails. "I'll do whatever you want. Take my blood! Or me! I don't care. Just leave Vail alone! Please!"

"It's always so much more fun when they beg, isn't it?" Ian smiled at Drake before turning back to me. He took a step forward, teasing me.

"So much fun," Drake agreed, smiling back.

He took two steps forward, wrapped his massive hands around Priscilla's head, and twisted her neck in one quick motion. The snap of her spine cracked through the air with a sickening sigh of relief.

"I'm a con man. Not a traitor," Drake muttered as Priscilla's limp body fell to the floor.

The silken web cuffs disintegrated from my arms.

I stretched my wrists, rubbing them while I tried to make sense of what had happened. Ian fell before me, twitching on the ground. A gust of wind howled down the corridor, barreling toward us in a violent vortex of thundering clouds. The door slammed against the wall, rattling off its hinges.

"Get down!" I yelled as the floor shook out from underneath me.

A streak of lightning flashed, spreading out like fingers through the smog until it reached Drake, curling around his neck in an electric grip. He instinctively reached up, grabbing the fiery tendrils and screaming before falling over.

"Drake!" Ian writhed on the floor, pushing himself up to his heels. He tore through the thick clouds that grew heavy as water, filling the room up with stale, suffocating air.

The storm brewed, growing more vicious by the second.

"I can't breathe! Vail! I can't breathe." Penelope gripped her throat and sucked in a breath of air before coughing. Her ivory skin purpled at her collar, stretching upward and settling into her gasping lips.

I stepped over Priscilla's body and reached for the key lying next to her palm. Her face was frozen in an evil grin, even in her death, and it would haunt me with a sickening dread forever. I forced the key in the cage lock and swung open the door. Penelope collapsed against me.

"You're safe. You're safe," I repeated as I pulled her along behind me.

Ian and Drake scrambled to their feet.

"Run!" Drake croaked, clutching his throat. "Go! Now!"

"But—" Ian pulled his brother's arm, dragging him across the floor.

"Just go!" Drake waved us away.

I swept Penelope into my arms and began to run.

The storm cracked behind us, chasing us down the long hall. The windows shattered as we passed, blowing bits of glass across our cheeks. Penelope shielded her eyes and curled into me, resting her head to my chest.

I reached the open front doors and leaped out as the thick tendrils of smog curled around my ankle. Penelope and I rolled across the porch, tumbled down the steps, and landed in the gravel drive.

"Drake. Drake!" Ian called, his voice distant.

I struggled to lift my head, but my neck gave way. I grunted, staring up at the moonlit sky. Penelope lay across me, breathing heavy.

"Vail?" Penelope's soft voice called out.

"Yeah?" I groaned. Every bone in my body ached.

"Take me home." Her voice broke.

"Okay." I swallowed hard, thinking Penelope didn't have a home to go to.

"He's okay! He's okay! Vail! Vail!" Ian yelled.

I lifted my head for a quick second and spotted my two brothers limping toward us.

CHAPTER NINE

PENELOPE

I ROLLED OFF OF VAIL AND FUMBLED TO MY FEET, STANDING up. I'd lost my shoes back in the manor along with my lie of a life and whatever other secrets Priscilla had taken to her grave. The terrifying realization that I wasn't who I'd thought I was—and worse, that my godmother wasn't who I'd thought she was—raked over me in a violent tremble.

"Are you okay?" Vail stood up and drew me in close.

I took a deep breath and bit back tears. Beside us, Ian and Drake lay on their backs, motionless.

"I'm going to tear it down," I whispered.

The manor rumbled, echoing a clap of thunder from the broken windows. Inside, the fog lifted.

"What?" he asked.

I planted my heels into the gravel, curling my toes atop the jagged rocks. A flash of anger spiraled up my spine and settled into my shoulders.

I gritted my teeth and repeated myself, "I said, I'm tearing it down."

A gust of wind howled down the corridor and out the front door, barreling past us. My hair whipped across my face.

"Penelope, I don't think that's a good idea. I think we need to go." Vail stepped back and curled his palms around my shoulders, studying my face.

I glanced sideways at the haunted house and began to hum. Thick, scaly vines erupted from the ground, slithering toward the manor and up the stone, wrapping its tendrils around the mansion with a spiky, thorny grip. Ian and Drake scrambled to their feet. The ground shook out from beneath me, but I continued humming.

"What's she doing?" Ian shouted.

I held my gaze on my work, admiring the ease at which I squeezed whatever life was left out of Priscilla's evil palace.

"Whatever she needs to do." Vail placed his palm on the small of my back, reassuring me to continue.

I shut my eyes tight and rose my hands in the air, setting the vines aflame. The manor shifted, collapsing in on itself in one long, defeated groan. I brought my fingertips to my flushed cheeks, feeling the heat of yet another fire that would forever blaze in my memory, and then I let go.

"Now, we can leave." I walked away.

The Bostwick brothers silently followed in my wake.

———

WHEN I ARRIVED BACK at the winery, most of the place looked as if nothing had happened. According to Vail, the rooms were left untouched. The Council had only destroyed the ballroom and labs.

"Why would they go in the labs if Priscilla had only hired them to scare me?" I asked as we made our way inside the winery and down toward the underground laboratory.

"If I were to guess, The Council knew a lot more than Priscilla thought. They had their suspicions, I'm sure. But Priscilla was the perfect excuse for them to look for evidence," Vail said.

"And they got it. They'll need to be dealt with next. After Finn." I set my mouth tight.

"Don't go on the attack. Let's let him explain himself first. Hell, you could have twisted me in thorns and set me to burn if there hadn't been protection spells on Priscilla's place. I saw the look in your eyes when you thought I was a traitor." Drake ran a hand through his hair.

"Yeah? And you knew about her telling The Council about the ball? You had to have. You were fucking her. You two seemed pretty close!" Ian snarled.

"I had no idea she told The Council shit! As I said, I'm not a fucking traitor. My relationship with her was lies and manipulation. On my part, and I guess hers!" Drake threw his hands in the air.

"You helped her though! You're a monster! You brought her innocent women to prey upon," I lashed out.

"I'm not a saint. I'm a fucking vampire." Drake stiffened. "And a reliable part of this team. It wasn't easy, conning a witch who tricked all of you. But if I'd had any idea that she planned to turn our party into a massacre, I'd have killed her the moment I found out."

"Let's talk about this later. We need more answers before we have a *sit down and share* meeting. No use in going back and forth until then. Let's keep our heads straight." Vail opened the door to the laboratory and let us pass.

The familiar blast of cold air and scent of chemicals instantly comforted me. It wasn't long ago that I'd worked as a lab rat in these rooms. My friends had stood by my side while I effortlessly stuck out my arm and donated to the Bostwick cause. A stab of guilt burrowed in my chest as memories of my fox, my goat, and my gargoyle flashed through my thoughts. Even Mirror Mirror wasn't visible. But Vail had reassured me on the car ride home that my team of misfits were safe, just like me.

I stuffed my losses deep down into the pit of my soul and took a deep breath. I had no time for feelings or to sit and ponder this new life I had to make. I couldn't rest until I finished the job, and even after learning all I'd learned in the last day, I had no idea what my future held or what my purpose was. I'd changed from being raised as a princess and serving my Prince Charming to becoming the antidote for vampirism, and now, I'd learned that, all along, I was an abomination.

"It's there, below the desk." Vail pointed to the floor. "That's his secret lab."

Ian and Drake scooted the metal desk to the side, revealing a large steel trapdoor.

"I know you're in there. We need to talk," Vail said as he walked over to a camera hanging in the corner.

The metal disk opened with a click. Finn pushed it to the side and climbed out. His hair shot out around his face as if we'd woken him from a deep sleep.

"You found her!" Finn ran to me, clasping his hands together under his chin as if I were an answer to a prayer. "And your hair! I like it! How did you do that?"

I stood motionless and unresponsive.

"Show us down there," Ian said, tipping his hat down the ladder and into the dark abyss.

"Why do you need to see down there?" Finn asked.

I glanced sideways at Vail. His black eyes sharpened.

"Priscilla is dead. You can't keep her secrets safe anymore. We know about the seeds and the princesses you're growing. You know, the ones like her." Vail wrapped his arm around me and pulled my hip to his. Our bodies clashed in an electric shock, zapping new life into my black soul.

I tensed, lifting my chin.

"Don't you dare look down," Vail would say as he swung me around the ballroom.

I felt nothing as I thought back to his constant reminder for me to keep my chin up. I'd left that woman on the dance floor. I would never stare at my slippers again.

Finn tugged his scraggly beard and began pacing the floor, moving with restless energy. "I don't know what you mean by *like her*. But I do know there were seeds Priscilla kept pushing me to alter."

"And?" Drake urged.

"And what?" Finn held his palms out and shrugged his shoulders. "That's not what's down there if that's what you're thinking. Every now and then, I'd show her clippings of whatever roots I could find to shut her up. But I never did what she asked, and I never asked questions about what she needed. Are you saying she wanted me to grow a princess? Like you?" Finn turned to me.

I chose my words carefully, weighing his version of the truth against Priscilla's. "Are you saying you had nothing to do with her experiments?"

"Is this a witch hunt? What the hell is this shit?" Finn's expression clouded in anger.

"She asked you a question," Drake said, inching toward the trapdoor.

"I took Priscilla's money and bribes and used it all on my selfish interests, combined with the cause. I got carried away in my scientific research and my lies. Priscilla thought I had rows of whatever the fuck plants I told her I was growing. I don't have a single thing down there that's alive." He cut his eyes to the trapdoor. "Yet."

"Why didn't you tell us you were working for her?" Vail asked.

"We were all working for her, right? She wanted to bridge dimensions to easily carry out her sick need for youth, so she could snatch her virgins herself. And we … well, we're vampires. She funded our project. Tit for tat. I have no regrets in lying to her and leading her on, and it looks like I was right to brush off her desires anyway. If all four of you are here, demanding answers with the look of death lingering behind your eyes, then I was justified in my initial reaction to her, which was to feed her bullshit."

"Mmhmm. Mind if I check?" Drake swiveled, making his way down the ladder before Finn could answer.

"By all means. But do not touch my projects. You might not understand them, but the hope for our cause lies down there." Finn watched as Drake disappeared down the tunnel. He turned his face to us. "Did you believe I'd betrayed you? Me?"

"There've been a lot of lies thrown around tonight. You'll excuse me if Priscilla told us you worked for her, and the first thought that crossed my mind was this secret lab you'd never told me about." Vail's voice hardened.

"I'm still me. I'm a Bostwick. But I have my own projects too—none of which anyone needed to know about. Trust me. It was better that way." Finn let out a long, audible breath.

"Is it the portals? Are you bridging the worlds?" I spoke up.

"No." He smirked. "That'll never happen, and Priscilla was an idiot to even entertain the idea. I wouldn't even try to break the code that keeps magic and the human world apart. Not only is it virtually impossible, but it's also dangerous. That's not the kind of danger I want to mess around with. Priscilla thought there was some type of portal in her basement, but it's complete rubbish, so I never believed it.

Besides, I can already straddle realms. There's nothing in it for me or any Bostwick. And if you haven't established it yet, I'm selfish."

My heart lurched in my chest. I knew linking the worlds through the code of magic was dangerous. But without that, I'd never see my friends again. I was doomed to stay an anomaly. A flash of wild grief ripped through me. I stumbled into Vail, gripping him tight and forbidding myself to fall.

A yelp came from down below. Finn looked away. I swayed on my feet.

"Ian, can you help Penelope upstairs? Clear the room of Mirror Mirror and the rest of the gang. Tell them she's okay but she needs privacy. Set them up in Leo's room, please." Vail pried my hands off of him and kissed my knuckles. "Go get cleaned up. I'll take care of this. You're here. You're safe. You're home."

I nodded, suddenly wilting. I wanted to tell Vail I wasn't home. I would never be home again. But instead, I grabbed on to Ian and let him help me to Vail's room.

MY TEETH CHATTERED under the sudden chill of hot water washing over my frozen skin. The shower pelted over my bruised body, numbing whatever pain I had left in me. My shoulders sagged under the weight of the world and the misery of knowing my family was so close yet so far away.

I scrubbed my head, working the knots in my hair out through my fingers and lathering the night's memories off of me and down the drain in blood-red whirls. I rubbed my temples, flinching at the cut on my brow. An earthy, woodsy scent drifted from behind me. Before I turned around, I knew he was there.

"I'll never get used to your silent reflexes. If I wasn't so tired, I'd have jumped through the roof." I faced Vail, stepping back so the water drenched him too. Hot droplets ricocheted off his massive shoulders, landing on my cheeks.

"I didn't mean to startle you. I just needed to be with you—here, alone. Away from the world for a bit." His eyes froze on my lips.

I cast my eyes down, suddenly aware of my damaged body.

He hooked his finger under my jaw and lifted my gaze to his before brushing his lips against my torn brow. "Chin up, buttercup."

"I'm trying." My skin flushed, burning under his touch, a rush of pink staining my cheeks.

"Are you still scared?" he asked, letting his hand fall to my breast.

My nipple hardened, instantly firming under his fingertips.

"No. Why do you say that?"

"Because I can feel your heartbeat thundering in your chest." He traced my lips with his thumb.

I parted my mouth and inhaled a deep breath.

"I feel you racing through my bloodstream. Your pulse is as erratic as a summer storm." A glint of wonder sparked in his eyes.

He pulled me to him, curling me into the rigid lines of his body. My breasts crushed against his taut, muscled chest. His erection bumped like steel against my thigh.

"It's you who's doing that to me." A wave of desire consumed me. "I need you."

I glided my hands down his back and over his pert ass before lowering myself to my knees. The shower streamed over my face as I looked up at Vail and began to suck his cock. His velvet skin melted in my mouth as I worked the crown of his cock. I slipped my hand under the soft flesh of his balls and gently teased them while drinking in the sweetness of him.

He peeked out from underneath his half-lidded gaze and sank back against the shower wall. I pumped my hand along his shaft in rhythm with my mouth as he urged me on with rapid, shallow breaths. Wild, untamed energy stirred inside me as I reached down and explored between my legs. I rocked against my fingers, circling my clit, as I swallowed his cock until I couldn't breathe. I squeezed my eyes shut and moaned.

He thrust his hands through my hair and pulled my head back, forcing me to look back up at him. His fangs hung low.

"Not yet," he growled as he shoved his hands under my arms and pulled me up.

He spun me around and pushed me up against the wall in one quick movement. His lips grazed the back of my neck, and he nipped the column of my throat. My breasts tingled against the cold shower tiles. I dragged my back hard against him.

"Then, take me to bed." My knees trembled. I pushed myself off the wall and faced him, aching with a need to feel him inside me.

He turned the shower off before lifting me in his arms and sliding the curtain back. As I straddled his waist, I bucked my hips in a driving need. The tip of his cock was poised at my entrance while he carried us to bed. He gently lay me down. I was soaking wet atop the sheets, but I didn't care. I wasn't cold. The icy flames of his flesh burned into me.

He crawled beside me, skimming his hand down my silken belly. "You're bruised. I'll not hurt you any more."

His lips seared a path down my chest, my breasts, my hips, and settled between my legs. I opened my mouth to argue my urgency, but his tongue feathered against my clit, and my brain collapsed to mush. He trailed his finger up my slit, spreading me while he slowly licked my wetness. I fluttered my eyes shut and raised my hips as he nibbled and kissed my clit. I arched my back and curled my toes with each flicker of his tongue. An urgent need ripped through me.

I writhed beneath him until he climbed atop me. I pressed my fingertips into his back, feeling his muscles tense beneath my touch. He caught my eye and held my gaze, easing himself inside me. His thick cock stretched me out, filling me up. I wrapped my legs around his trembling waist and nestled into him, resting my forehead against his shoulder.

"Oh fuck." I let out a breath.

My fevered skin fused against his flesh as he slid upward against me, driving his hips into mine. I lifted myself, matching his rhythm, and stroked my fingers down the length of his back before gripping his ass, forcing him deeper into me. His breath came in long, throaty moans.

"I need to feed," he groaned, baring his fangs. He threw his head back and hesitated.

"Do it," I pleaded. "I need to feel it."

I raised my mouth to his chest and grazed my lips on his collar. He quivered, thrusting into me with rough, slow strokes. I arched my back and rocked against him. An ache whipped through me, rising like fire.

"Fucking drain me," I commanded, jerking my head to the side and exposing my neck.

His abs tightened. He closed his eyes and raked his fangs over my throat, searching for the pulsing hollow of my collar, and sank his teeth in viciously. Waves of pleasure racked my body, throbbing in sync with my pulse. My blood spilled out inside his mouth while he spilled out inside me. I wrapped myself around him and cried out, exhaling with relief. I spread my thighs wide as he gave one final push before slowing his pace.

He opened his eyes again and smiled. I relaxed into a puddle underneath him, hypnotized by his touch.

"I missed you so much," he said, planting kisses on my brow, my nose, my lips before pausing to whisper, "I'll never let you go again."

"You don't have to," I said, nuzzling into him.

He rolled off of me and propped himself up on an elbow. "You're here to stay. I'll keep you safe."

My thoughts filtered back to The Council—a problem we'd yet to deal with. I waited until my pulse quieted.

"But what about—" I started.

He pressed his lips to mine, silencing me.

CHAPTER TEN

VAIL

AFTER PENELOPE HAD ARRIVED BACK AT BOSTWICK, SHE SLEPT for days. Trevor paced outside of her room morning and night, but the fox could not return to his owner. They would never be reunited unless something happened to fix the princess's predicament.

"She's safe," I told her companions before quietly closing her door. "You can't see her, so stay out here. She might smell you or something and get even more depressed."

"Depressed?" Mirror Mirror asked.

I'd hung him outside in the hall. I didn't need any enchanted mirrors cracking jokes at me about fucking a ghost.

"Of course. That's why she's been sleeping and barely eating. She learned her life was a lie, and it's going to take time for her to come to grips with it. I promise I'll keep you all up-to-date."

"One out of ten." Grump hiccuped.

"Sorry, buddy. I wish I had better news. I've got some

business to take care of. Why don't you all go do normal woodland-creature things?" I brushed the hair out of my eyes in Mirror Mirror's reflection.

"And what about me? I guess I'll just hang around then. No one to talk to, nothing to do. Can you at least move me to a better location if I'm not going to be in your bedroom, scoring you on your sex moves with the invisible?" Mirror Mirror said.

"Ugh, yeah. Actually, great idea!" I pulled the mirror off the wall and headed downstairs. "Follow me, everyone."

Otto missed a step and tumbled down the stairs, reaching the bottom floor before the rest of us. His wings flapped slowly, pulling him back to his feet. Trevor flicked his tail in the gargoyle's direction.

"This place you're taking us to, does it have any wine?" Grump asked, hobbling on his hooves.

"You know this is a winery, right?" I perched Mirror Mirror on my hip and patted the goat's head.

We wound our way down a narrow hall and into the basement.

"Welcome to the lab, boys. Don't touch anything." I turned, pushing the door open with my back.

The lab had been cleaned spotless, but the cooling chamber's shelves were as empty as ever. We were running out of blood.

"What's this?" Finn asked, emerging from his office and throwing the tails of his lab coat behind him.

"Your interns." I hung Mirror Mirror beside the old cot.

The last time Penelope had lain on the mattress was when she donated blood before passing out. She'd breathed deeply in a peaceful slumber, her golden curls falling to the side. I smiled, thinking about her innocence.

"I think I'd rather watch you make a fool of yourself in bed," Mirror Mirror muttered.

"How will I get any work done in here with varmints running around?" Finn threw his hands in the air.

Otto hissed and stuck out his tongue.

"It's only for a little while. They're restless upstairs. I promise they won't be in your way. Just give them a job."

"What the hell can they do for me?" Finn asked.

I side-eyed the fox, the goat, the gargoyle, and the mirror.

"I can test your wine," Grump said between chews. The wrinkled top sheet on the cot hung from his mouth.

"Trevor and Otto are pretty good guards. They can stand outside the premises and make sure The Council or anyone else isn't nearby. Grump can ..." I scratched my head. "Grump can survey the grapes. I'll let Ian know he's to help in the vineyards. And Mirror Mirror can offer you his company."

"So, why do they need to be down here?" Finn folded his arms.

To watch you, but I quickly banished the thought. The recent turn of events had me paranoid of everyone and anyone, even my own brother, who I'd known for damn near a century.

"Because they need space from Penelope. They can smell her. I told you, they're restless. Until I can figure this thing out, I need to keep them away for a bit. This *riding dimensions* thing is bullshit."

Finn cleared his throat and looked away. "I'll be in my lab." He swiveled on his heels and made his way back to his office before disappearing under his trapdoor.

"Gee, who pissed in his Project X?" Grump spit out the sheet.

"He's overworked, is all. Go on up to the vineyard, you three. I'll be right behind you." I shooed the animals out of the lab before turning to Mirror Mirror. "Do me a favor."

"Thought so. What is it? Another traitor in our midst?" Mirror Mirror asked.

"I don't think so. But I get a dreadful feeling down here."

"You're telling me. The moment you opened the door, this crack across my face splintered. And now, I have to live here. Broken." He huffed, fogging his glass.

"You don't have to live here. Just stay here for a bit. Keep your eyes and ears open. I'll check in periodically for any reports," I reassured Mirror Mirror, walking backward.

"But what am I looking for?" he called out.

"Everything."

I hurried up the stairs and out the door, catching up to the animals.

The full moon hung low in a cloudless sky. The night grew chilly, but it wasn't unbearable. Our grapevines still needed to be checked and tended throughout the winter months. We'd cut the daytime handlers' hours after the massacre, leaving Ian and Drake with more work and less time. Wine tastings had stopped entirely under the guise of renovations. I hadn't had the motivation to gather new investors. And once word got out about the doomed investor ball, I doubted anyone would want to mingle with our cause.

I jogged over to the barn, passing rows of tethered vines, scraggly and bare. Otto, Grump, and Trevor bounced off into the distance. A rush of voices erupted from behind the wooden barn doors. I swiftly pressed my back to the side of the barn and listened.

"Bruno isn't going to take that for an answer. We'll need more information. We know you burned her and her manor. A lone wolf saw you," a voice snarled.

"Look, Antonio, we admit it was us. We caught Priscilla doing some ... really evil things. When we found out and confronted her, she threatened us. We defended ourselves, and that's that," Ian said.

"Ian's right. I know Bruno was close to her, but he wouldn't have hesitated to kill her either if his life was in danger."

"What types of things was she doing?" Antonio's voice grew husky.

I flung myself off the side of the barn and burst through the door.

"Gentlemen." I nodded at the werewolf sheriff, Antonio, and his pack.

"Oh, Vail. Now, maybe we'll get somewhere." Antonio rolled his eyes and leaned sideways, propping himself on the side of a wine barrel. "I take it, you're in charge now with Leo gone? We offer our condolences, by the way. But I'm here on witch business. Tell me what happened at Priscilla's mansion."

"Yeah, sorry about that." I kneaded my shoulder.

"I need a lot more information than that, friend. Why'd you murder her?" Antonio creased his brows. He wore a rugged, somber profile. His graying beard lay unkempt and scattered across his face in an uneven pattern. Tufts of thick silver hair stuck out from beneath the collar of his uniform.

I weighed the question before answering, "Priscilla was killing ... the young and innocent. Not just virgin maidens who had stumbled onto the wrong path. She was breeding to kill. She tried to harvest life for only that purpose."

Antonio let out a howl, followed by the echoes of his pack.

"I'll let Bruno know. He's a dragon, but he's not a killer. Not unless he has to be. Gold means more to him than life. He'd rob a bank before he robbed a life. I'm sure he'll have questions for you though. But I trust you. This one here though"—Antonio tipped his head toward Drake—"not so much."

The younger wolves shrugged at Drake. I'd thought they

had become friends over the last few months. But wolves had a hierarchy, and whatever Antonio said or thought was final.

"I await any questions your boss has for me. We've nothing to hide. But learning what we've learned, it's not something you want in your head, if you know what I mean."

"Understandable." Antonio nodded, motioning for his pack to leave.

The werewolves filed out the barn door. He followed on their heels before swiveling and turning back.

"Ah, what about Penelope? I noticed The Council got her home too. But she was here, right? Is she here? And okay?" he asked.

"She's here and okay. Thanks for asking." I inched forward and dipped my head.

"She seems like a good lady. She and Gertie." Antonio bit his lip with a row of sharp teeth.

I didn't bother to tell him about Penelope's godmother. That would require energy I didn't have, so I only gave him a dismissive nod before he disappeared through the door.

"Phew. That went a lot better than I'd imagined." Ian let out a deep breath.

"I knew she wasn't *banging* close with Bruno. Just business close." Drake dragged his feet to the side of the barn, propping one on a bench and tying his shoelace.

"That's because you were banging her," I said.

He dusted off his hands and looked at me. His expression grew serious, but a twitch of his lips gave him away. "For the cause."

"For the cause." I laughed, feeling somewhat back to normal even if only for a slight moment.

I SPENT NEARLY two hours catching up on tasks in the barn with my brothers. We made small talk about life, work, and the critters guarding the vineyards outside. I told them how Finn had reacted to Mirror Mirror and friends in his lab, and they laughed. When I asked Drake what Finn had stored down in his secret lab, he only shook his head and shivered.

"That bad, eh?" I asked.

"Body parts. From ogres to gnomes and maybe humans. I don't know. I didn't care to stay long and find out. I guess he's extracting DNA or something. I've never been the nerdy science type, so who knows?" Drake lifted a bag of tools and set them on the shelf.

"Disgusting. We're sure he didn't kill for those?"

"I don't think Finn would do that. Besides, he's always down there. When would he have the time to roam the night, murdering folks?" Ian asked.

"No clue. Anyone seen any finger delivery services at the door? Maybe a *toe* truck?" I stretched my arms over my head and yawned.

Ian and Drake roared with laughter.

"Toe-tally!" Drake shook his head.

"I missed this." Ian dropped his gaze to the floor.

"Me too. We're slowly getting there and back to normal. We'll figure it out." I brushed dirt from my knees and pulled my collar from my neck, fanning the layer of dust off of me.

"And then we'll figure The Council out," Drake growled.

"Yep. There's always more work to do. Until then, I've got the fox and gargoyle pacing outside, acting as security guards. I'm keeping them busy. I'm going to check on Penelope," I said, ducking out of the barn and waving good-bye.

"Trevor and Otto are on guard duty? Eesh. So, if we hear any fox screams, it means, run for the hills!" Ian joked.

"What does the fox say anyway?" I called over my shoulder.

"Hikey ho or some shit." Drake shrugged.

I jogged back to the house in a fit of giggles and newfound joy until I reached the back patio. Penelope stood, staring off into the forest. A wild look sparked in her eyes.

"What're you doing out here? You should be asleep! It's well after midnight." I rushed to her side, cradling her in my arms.

"I keep thinking of all Gertie did. She killed herself for me. I can't fault her for lying all those years if she was only trying to protect me. I'll never understand a mother's love." Her voice shook.

I buried my hands in her hair and took a deep breath. Her scent filled my lungs with the comfort only she could give me. "Yes, you will." I sighed.

"No, I won't." She shivered her soft curves into my chest.

"Don't you want children? Don't you want to marry someone and have babies?" I stepped back, searching her eyes.

"I can't have children. I can plant and grow them. Or at least, a queen can if she's lucky. But I'm not going to be a queen anymore. I'm not even a princess. And plus, I ... I only want you and your babies. And that won't happen because you don't work like that either."

"You what?" I asked, taking a step back.

"I didn't say anything. Nope, not me." She wiped a smile from her face.

"That's not what I heard. You want vampy princess babies —or whatever it is we'd make. Probably some little girl who would one day rule the entire world with butterflies and dragons. She'd be adaptable like that."

She threw her head back and laughed, displaying her familiar dazzling smile that I remembered from before our world had changed.

"I love you so much," she said, wrapping her arms around me and pulling my hips to meet hers.

I grabbed her by the waist and swung her around before setting her back down.

"I love you too. And I have for a long"—I kissed her forehead—"long"—I kissed the tip of her nose—"long"—I pressed my lips to hers—"time." I brushed her hair from her neck, revealing two bruised puncture wounds. I gently nuzzled the marks I'd left on her.

"Then, why the hell didn't you tell me?" She playfully smacked my ass.

"I'm a chickenshit, of course. I was waiting on you," I lied. I'd planned on telling her the moment I thought she could handle it. But I'd never dreamed she would be the first to take a big leap of faith and put herself out there.

"No, you aren't. You saved me. You're my hero." She lifted herself on her toes and curled her arm around my waist before putting her hand in mine.

"Ready?" I hooked my arm around her.

"One, two, three. One, two, three, three," she said as I twirled her through the vines.

Moonlight washed over her ivory skin, bathing it in a breathtaking glow. My chest spasmed with a slight heartbeat. I pulled her close and turned my face to the night sky as a shooting star soared behind Penelope, causing me to miss a step in our dance. Penelope hadn't seen the twinkle, and I didn't dare mention it to her. If Gertie were watching over us, she'd let it be known soon enough. But for now, I didn't want my princess thinking of painful memories. I wanted to stay like this, happy and dancing with her forever. I closed my eyes and made a wish.

I SENT Penelope back up to bed while I sorted a few things in the lab. She skipped off in a series of twirls and leaps while humming an upbeat tune. I thought back to when she'd first danced in the ballroom. Every step she had taken burst a flower from the wooden floor, and butterflies had flown from under her dress. She looked as radiant now as she had then.

"What the hell were you doing, twirling around here like that for?" Grump said, nudging my leg and startling me. His pupils were as big as saucers, and he reeked of our Black Label wine.

"I was dancing with Penelope." I reached down, patting his head.

"Oh. I thought I'd drunk too much."

"You probably did."

"It happens." He hiccuped. "Wait a minute. You said she was dancing?"

"Yep." I shoved my hands in my pockets and rocked back on my heels, grinning.

"What's gotten into her?"

"I guess her grief is lifting. I hope so anyway. Come on. I'll walk you to bed."

The drunk goat stumbled, tangling his hooves in a way I'd thought was impossible.

"I think you'd better carry me."

"Right," I said.

I whistled, calling Trevor's and Otto's attention. The fox and gargoyle trotted toward us. Otto shook his massive head at Grump as I scooped the goat into my arms and carried him inside. I squinted at the blinding halogen lights in the basement.

No matter the time of day or night, the machines in the lab kept running. I didn't even know exactly what the machines did or how they operated. I didn't need to know those things either. Finn held the role of our resident scientist, and his brilliance kept the place going. But I'd learned people could carry some things too far, and these days, my brother's erratic behavior made it seem as if he had gone mad.

I tiptoed to the cot, shooting a glance into the windowed office Finn used, but I saw no signs of him. No doubt, he was working below deck on the projects Drake had mentioned. I didn't want details on his work—as long as it didn't go against our vampire code, which was pretty damn ethical for vampires. I hadn't tasted human blood in years.

"Vail. Psst. Vail," Mirror Mirror whispered.

Grump had fallen limp in my arms, snoring in thick, croaking gasps, and I set the goat on the cot and covered him with a sheet. Trevor and Otto hopped up onto the bed and curled in next to him.

"What is it?" I whispered back, turning to look at my reflection in Mirror Mirror.

"I think Penelope came down here. Finn spoke with someone I couldn't see. It had to be her."

"Really?" I leaned on the edge of the mattress and folded my arms. "What did he say?"

"It was hard to follow, considering it sounded like a one-sided conversation. But I heard him mention The Council, and he nodded a lot. He talked about heart specimens, and he promised more than once that he didn't have anything to do with seeds. He also asked her a lot of questions."

"Like?"

"Like specifics on how she vanished and what she felt when she performed dark magic. Science stuff. He said being born of the sunflower might not be the cure, but her coming from a cursed seed is more likely the answer."

I rubbed my temples. "Okay. Thanks for letting me know." I turned to leave.

"But wait! There's more!"

I groaned.

"I think he took her blood. Like, a lot. They went into his office, and he shut the door. When he came out, he had jars of it." Mirror Mirror's eyes snapped toward the full top shelf inside the glass cooling chamber.

"Shit." I swallowed hard. "When was this?"

"About an hour ago."

I scratched my head and thought of the change in Penelope's mood. Something had happened in her conversation with Finn. Her joy was contagious and almost hopeful. I'd thought she'd rounded the corner of grief, but the dozens of vials of fresh blood perched atop the shelf only told me she had still been searching for answers, and instead of coming to me, she had gone to Finn. A hard knot formed in the pit of my stomach.

"I'll find out what's going on. Just do me a favor and keep your eyes and ears open."

I left the laboratory in a state of confusion. The confidence I'd had when I made my wish suddenly vanished as quickly as my princess.

CHAPTER ELEVEN

PENELOPE

I SAT ON THE SECOND-FLOOR BALCONY, CUPPING MY HANDS around a warm coffee mug, savoring the sunrise. The vineyards glistened with a mid-season frost. The brothers had spent all night spraying the vines to avoid damage to their varietals.

Since I'd returned, I watched. I listened. I learned. I soaked up every bit of information to one day help Bostwick out and contribute to the winery. But Vail kept me at a distance. His mood had changed over the last few days from joy over having me back to caution when I asked questions.

He'd told me meddling in the affairs of vampires would prove more dangerous than I realized. My ambition to help in the winery wasn't practical. I was a threat to The Council, and once they figured out my whereabouts, they'd kill me off this time. I couldn't stay much longer. Finn had told me about the vampire he'd caught drinking my blood, who had gotten away during the attack on Bostwick. Vail had a suspicion The Council was lying low to plan another attack.

But I had a better idea. We could attack them first.

I dipped my nose into my mug and inhaled before taking a long, slow sip of my drink, peering over the rim, past the forest where I'd once lived. The treetops sparkled like a winter wonderland, full of magic and mystery. But I knew those woods. Only nightmares and memories I'd like to forget lurked in my old forest. I hadn't set foot in there since I'd been back even though the woods called to me. The trees bowed in the wind, splitting a path to let me through. But I wasn't ready to face my demons. Bostwick had become my home now, and I'd tirelessly work to find my new place in life.

Life.

The word hung in my thoughts.

I finished my coffee and set down the mug. The sun rose over the horizon, spreading its rays over the chilled earth. I stood, leaning against the railing. The sunshine warmed my cheeks with familiar comfort. I soaked in the light of dawn for the rest of the morning, saying my good-byes and filing away the warmth I knew I'd miss before I headed back inside and into an unknown future.

I tiptoed across the room and slid back under the sheets, nestling up to Vail. He stirred next to me. His cool skin rubbed against mine, sucking the heat from my body. My heartbeat pounded in my chest so loud that I wondered if Vail could hear it. I knew, especially after all the feeding he had done last night, he could feel it too. The more he drank from me, the more his vampire strength vanished. He'd warned me that he needed to slow down and fight tempta-tion. He wanted to protect me from The Council when they showed up—and they *would* show up sooner or later.

The brothers had nightly discussions and brainstorming sessions on how best to approach their vampire enemies. But for my protection, Vail never let me in on any planning.

Instead, he kept me hidden, and I didn't like being tucked away in a forest or a basement. I didn't want to hide anymore.

Theo had cast me away out of shame, and instead of wallowing in my days as an old maid, I'd risen to the challenge and gained retribution. Granted, I wasn't the one who had ripped his head off, but at least he was only a shadow in my memory and a closed chapter in my fairy tale.

"Vail? Are you awake?" I trailed my palm down his broad shoulder, tracing my finger along the ridges of his bicep to his palm.

"Yes. I couldn't sleep. You okay?" He rolled over and propped himself on his elbow. A strand of unruly hair fell into his face.

"I'm okay. Just thinking about how it must be hard for you to adjust, is all." I brushed the hair from his eyes.

"What do you mean?" he asked.

"I mean, you adjusting to my time and all and trying to sleep some at night."

"Well, I'm not sleeping." He laughed.

"That's exactly what I mean." I took a deep breath and focused on lowering my heart rate. My thundering pulse was going to give away my proposal before I could even sputter out the words.

Vail sat up in bed. A deep crease stretched across his brows.

"What's on your mind?" His voice was already tinged with disapproval. He could sense my unease.

I sat up and wrung my hands. "I'm just saying, it doesn't have to be this way, you know?"

"What way?" He pinched the bridge of his nose and squeezed his eyes shut. His posture tensed.

"I want to go home, Vail."

"But this is your home now." He opened his eyes again but avoided my gaze.

I swallowed a lump in my throat and steadied my breathing. "I mean, I want to see magic again. I want to see Trevor, Grump, Otto, and even Mirror Mirror. I don't want to be in this world anymore. There's nothing for me here. I want to go home."

"But you can't. It's impossible. I'm sorry. I wish I could help," he lied.

"You can, and you know it."

"I'm not sure how. I have no spells. I have no magic. I have nothing. I'm only a vampire."

"You can turn me." The words spilled out of me like lightning, charging the air with dangerous energy and shocking us both.

Vail drew in a breath and squared his shoulders. The tendons in his neck sharpened as he tightened his jawline. His pupils dilated with suppressed fury.

He spoke to me in a careful, controlled tone, "You know, after I deal with this Council mess, I'll be actively trying to turn myself back human. To live in your world. Most of Bostwick wants that. It's been the plan all along, Penelope. You don't want to be one of us." He held his palms to the air before sliding out of bed and wiggling into a pair of pants he had left lying on the floor. His chest muscles tensed, growing as rigid as carved marble.

"I do want to be one of you." I pushed myself out of bed and wrapped a thick robe around me. I threw the hood over my head, tucking in my black-streaked hair and shrinking myself into the oversize garment. If I could hide inside of it, I would. There were only a handful of times I'd caught sight of the real vampire in Vail. This was one of them.

"No," he grunted. "This is Finn's doing. He planted this idea in your head. I had a feeling about it."

"No! I'm capable of making my own decisions, you know. You think because I'm a princess, I can't think for myself?" I stomped over to him and drew myself up to my full height. My head barely reached his shoulders.

He put his palms in the air, stopping me. "That's not what I said!"

"Gertie always told me she wished princesses were taught independence and how to take care of themselves. She believed we were capable of more than just summoning butterflies and whispering sweet nothings to our Prince Charming. She believed in me, and I thought I was letting her down by not studying my spells hard enough and disappearing into the human world. But that had been her plan all along. She protected me to the end. She did it for me. And I believe in me too. I'm not going to let myself fall into the hands of danger when my godmother fought and lost the battle to save me. Her life was worth more than a deadly failure. And my life is worth more than fucking sunshine and rainbows. I'm not a princess anymore. I never was. I don't know what I am. But I do know what I'm capable of. I—"

"And you think turning into a vampire is going to magically make you happy? How can you even think that? Why would you believe that when you know my brothers and I are trying *not* to be vampires?" he said, interrupting me.

"Maybe if you had let me finish, you would know." I clenched my fists to my sides and gritted my teeth. I wasn't a vampire yet, but I already felt the sting of venom in my throat.

Vail fell onto the edge of the bed and sighed. He propped his elbows on his knees and buried his face in his palms, avoiding my gaze.

"Go on then," he said, his voice muffled through his hands.

"Finn and I have been discussing how to get to The Council and end them. We have a semi-plan."

"Semi? These aren't run-of-the-mill vampires. These are elite, centuries-old villains who will destroy you with one bite. You need to have a better plan than a *semi*." He threw his hands in the air.

"Are you going to let me speak?" A flash of heat flushed through my body, settling into my chest.

"Sorry. I just don't like the thought of you throwing your life away. Forgive me for being bitter about it," he spat out the words and snapped his eyes to mine.

"I can help get rid of The Council. You saw my talents. Imagine the scale they would be if I were as strong and powerful as a vampire. Finn and I have come up with a few different scenarios, but more than likely, we'll need to inject The Council with my blood somehow. They'll weaken after a concentrated dose of me turns them back human. Then, I can finish them off with one quick curse. Afterward, you'll use my blood to turn back to a human. If that's what you want."

"And you? You would turn human too?"

"I don't know what I want. I'm not prepared to make that decision yet. All I know is, I want to see my family and be back home. I want to fix this and feel safe again, so I can move on, in whatever life that might be." I bit my lip and inched forward.

Vail rubbed his chest. "I love you, Penelope. I don't want to lose you again."

"You don't have to."

"I do. Unless we're both human or both vampires." He rose from the bed and paced the room. The wooden floor-boards creaked with each of his lumbering steps. "Fuck. I knew after I made my wish to be with you forever, it was a mistake. I wanted us to turn human, have babies or adopt

145

them. Whatever we had to do to start a family and have a future. I didn't mean for you to become a vampire and us live our days in grim and lonely immortality. But after I made the wish, it crossed my mind." He ran his hands through his hair before letting them fall to his sides.

"What do you mean, you made a wish?" I folded my arms over my chest and shifted my feet.

"The other night, when we danced, I saw a twinkle."

"Gertie." I swayed slightly.

"We don't know that."

"I know that."

"How?"

"Because I saw a twinkle too. The night before. And I wished for the same," I said.

He paused, swiveling around and staring at me.

"What exactly did you wish for?" he asked.

"I asked to return home, so I could be with you and my friends forever. That's when the idea of turning hit me. I went to Finn the next day and confirmed it. It will work. One of our twinkles, or both, had to have been Gertie. She's still looking out for me, Vail. And this is obviously the path I'm supposed to take."

"Your godmother saved you from danger. You really think she wants you to live your life as a ruthless vampire?" He peered down at me.

The reality of his words stung but not enough for me to second-guess my choice.

I threw my shoulders back and stared him straight in the eye. "You didn't know my godmother like I did. I think she wants her little princess to emerge as a queen. The vampire journey is just one step closer to my destiny."

Vail flinched. "You're not the same princess I met, twirling in the woods."

"I know."

"You're much more." He took two strides toward me and hooked his arm around my waist. "I don't question your plan because I don't believe in you. I question it because I do. You're capable of great things. Big things. Scary things. And if I'm honest, maybe even evil things."

"Hey!" I pulled back and playfully swatted his shoulder.

"I saw what you did to Priscilla's place. You wore the same wild look in your eyes as you had back at The Cave when you set it on fire. You have something in you that's untamed. If you're going to play with fire, you need to know how to extinguish flames too." He searched my eyes.

"That untamed part of me is who I am, planted in me since birth. I'm sure I can wield it properly now that I know what powers reside inside of me. But I can't use them unless I'm on your level and in your realm. I don't belong here."

"And if it changes your blood? What then? You're the only cure for vampirism that we know of. What will happen to our cause if you change?"

"Finn has enough of my blood to last for a long while. Besides, we've been experimenting with mixing my blood and vampire venom. So far, there haven't been any *negative* changes." I looked away.

"But?"

"My cells reacted with the venom in a way he hadn't seen before. You know the untamed part of me you mentioned?"

He nodded.

"It becomes more … powerful. Like, way more powerful. My cells hardened and grew stronger. They were invincible to fire, drowning, poison, anything he threw at them. Of course, he still has tons of tests to do, but don't worry about my blood weakening. That test has performed exceptionally well. He even injected himself with the mixture and felt a faint pulse. You can still return to your human form, Vail."

He rubbed his jaw and drew me in close. I buried my face

in his chest, took a deep breath, and inhaled his woodsy scent. He smelled like home.

"It sounds like you've already planned this," he said.

I lifted myself on my toes and muttered into his neck, "It's done. I just want you to be the one who takes me home."

"You don't know what you're asking for." He turned his head, grazing his lips against my cheek.

"That's my choice to make." I pressed my mouth to his and stopped him from discussing it further.

THE AIR in the lab grew cold, chilling me to the bone. Ian, Drake, Finn, and Vail stood, surrounding the medical cot I'd lain on several times before. But this time was different. Restraints were tied around my wrists and ankles, bolting me to the bed. A tangle of wires was spread across my chest, hooking me up to a continually beeping monitor.

"The only thing I can do is pain management. But even then, it doesn't take your pain completely away." Finn held a syringe in the air and thumped it a few times.

I bit down on my lip and held out my arm. The pulsing on the monitor quickened.

"Give her a double dose if you have to. Whatever it takes." Vail covered my forehead with his palm and brushed my hair back.

He carried the weight of the world in his eyes. His worry rubbed off on me.

"I think she's tougher than she lets on. She can handle it." Ian grinned, exposing his boyish dimples.

"Well, after this, I certainly won't be about fluffy bunnies and sunshine anymore." I grabbed Vail's hand and squeezed as Finn sank the needle into the crook of my elbow. The medicine burned, slowly spreading fire throughout my veins. I buckled in response.

"Hold still. You'll only feel it for a minute," Finn said.

My breath caught in my throat.

"That's because you'll no longer be able to bask in the sun's rays. You won't be sunshine anymore, Sunflower Princess," Vail said, clenching his jaw and looking away.

"Ah, now, come on. She's still your sunshine. Look at the bright side!" Drake tried and failed to lighten the mood.

"There's no bright side," Vail muttered, interrupting him. His profile grew rigid.

"I get to be with you for eternity." I fluttered my eyes at him. But even I couldn't hide my fear.

"At the cost of your life. You never know how precious it is until you lose it. But you're about to find out, I suppose." Vail stroked my hair and leaned down, kissing the top of my head.

"I can always come back. Who knows how I'll feel? Let's think of it as temporary for now. Finn has plenty of my blood. I can cure myself anytime if I choose. And so can all of you."

"After we take care of The Council." Ian's eyes snapped to Vail's.

"Aye. We've work to do, boys ... and girl. Or should I say, soon-to-be sister?" Finn smiled.

A brittle, stifling tension filled the air with dread as we awaited my death.

The monitor pulsed in a series of quick bursts.

Beep, beep, beep, beep.

I could only nod.

"And you're absolutely sure? Any second-guessing your-self?" Ian stood at my feet, patting my ankle.

"I'm sure." The words fell out of my mouth. My heart thundered in my chest, aching against my rib cage like it was fighting to escape. I couldn't blame it. I was actively preparing to kill it.

"Fuck! This isn't right. I can't believe I'm doing this to you." Vail rubbed his palm over his eyes.

"But I want to go home." I reached up, pulling his hand back down to me. I needed to hang on to him.

He'd stayed as my constant throughout all the bullshit I'd been through in the last few months.

"I know; I know." He shook his head and glanced at something next to him that I couldn't see.

"Are they here?" I asked, scanning the room for any signs of my family. I thought I'd detected a whiff of my smelly fox, but my imagination grew delirious with fright, the longer I stalled the procedure.

"Yes. They're all waiting. Mirror Mirror says, 'On with the show, bitch,' " Drake said. His voice was charged with energy. I would soon replace his position as the youngest Bostwick vampire.

I laughed.

"Bastard. Tell him I'll see them soon." I took a deep breath and gulped back the fear rising in my throat. My eyes darted around the room, refusing to settle on anything. Anxiety coursed through my veins, scattering my thoughts into a skittish mess.

Vail sat on the edge of the cot and leaned down, covering my shaking body with his and soothing me. He held me tight and whispered, "I love you."

"I love you too." I clung to him.

He pulled back, placed his hand on my chest, feeling for my heartbeat, and closed his eyes. I knew he was filing it in his memory.

"Vail?" I asked.

"Hmm?" He opened his eyes. They were wet with tears.

My blood still lingered in him, giving him subtle human traits.

I swiped my thumb across his cheek and wiped a tear away. His pupils dilated wide enough for me to watch my reflection in them. But the woman looking back at me wasn't a princess anymore. She was a warrior, and my battle had only just begun.

"Bite me," I said in a firm and final tone. I tilted my chin and exposed my neck. "Bite me."

He wasted no time. In one quick motion, Vail's fangs sank deep into my neck with a searing pain that took my breath away—literally. My body seized under the weight of him.

I began to gasp, drowning in a room full of air.

"You're okay. You're going to be okay. Hey, look at me." Vail clamped his fingers over my trembling chin and steadied my jaw. "Don't look away. Eyes on me, okay? One, two, three. One, two, three, three. We got this. I'm here. We're in this together. Hold on to me."

He tried to hold me down, but I writhed against the restraints, rubbing my ankles and wrists into a bloody mess.

His venom shot through my bloodstream like flames, burning up everything inside me and turning it into hot ash. I gnashed my teeth at Vail, who swiftly pulled away from me. Drake and Ian held down my legs, and Finn grabbed my wrists. The restraints buckled, rubbing my skin raw underneath.

The beeping on the monitor grew faster.

"This doesn't seem normal!" Vail shouted over my screams.

"Give it time!" Finn shouted back.

I arched my back, nearly snapping my spine in half as I wrestled to break free. I forgot where I was, what I was doing, and who I was with. I only needed to survive.

I kicked a leg in the air, tearing it from the restraint.

"I told ya, she's tough. Like a fucking bull!" Ian pinned my legs down underneath his chest.

The monitor's beeping became erratic.

It's not working.

This is it. I'm going to die.

Faint outlines of familiar faces faded into view before vanishing again. A ball of fire grew inside my chest, blazing me from the inside out. I screamed, breaking loose from my wrist restraints and wildly flinging my arms around. I knocked Drake across the room. His back crashed into the wall behind him.

"Fuck!" Finn said, grabbing another syringe and jabbing it into my arm.

My brain turned to mush.

A chaotic mix of memories and delusions flooded my thoughts.

The room began to spin in circles, the way it had when Vail swung me through the air at the ball. Then, I saw bright lights as I rode the chandelier down in a dazzling display of glory. Vail picked me up and kissed me. He tasted like Bostwick Black Label. Gertie watched my performance with wet eyes. She flicked her wand and sent dozens of sunflower petals falling over the ballroom, whirling down like little snowflakes. Priscilla stood beside Gertie, wrinkling her nose. Icicles formed at my feet.

"Can you hear me? Penelope! Penelope!" Vail shouted. "Do something, Finn!"

I watched Elly, Henry, and Fritzi eating pizza at the dinner table, laughing. Henry held up a cup of coffee and gave me an invisible toast. His shoes blinked in tune with the monitor's spotty beeps.

Pervy Pumpkin rolled under my feet and tripped me, sending me down a rabbit-hole-like trapdoor at the bottom of our cottage. I fell through the Bostwick laboratory and landed in Poppycock, at the feet of my headless ex-fiancé, Prince Theo.

"I can't do anything! She has to pull through it herself!" Finn yelled.

My mind jumped to my younger self. I watched as I attended princess school. I twirled my skirts and summoned a rain cloud. I should have summoned a rainbow.

My mind jumped again. I was a young child now, skipping along the rocks in a nearby creek. Layers of mud covered my feet.

The school's headmaster scolded me, "Princesses don't get dirty."

I sent the rain cloud to hang over his head for the next six months.

I zipped through a series of flashes and bubbles and fire. The Bostwick winery crumbled. My cottage crumbled, Priscilla's mansion crumbled. And in the ashes, Gertie sat, tending a bloom that, despite the mountain of death, grew from it all—me. She raked her hand across the ash and hummed to the sprouting sunflower. I sang back.

And then my mind went blank.

One final wave of pain ripped through me as my heart struggled to escape the empty void overtaking it. But it lost the fight and withered away. I tossed about, breathing out scorching breaths until my body grew limp. My mouth ached with a slicing, sharp pain. The beeping monitor slowed, paused, and stopped altogether.

Beep. Beep. Beeeeeep. Beep. Beeeeeeeep.

"Penelope? You in there?" Vail leaned in closer. His shouts cut through the room's sudden heavy silence.

I blinked, focusing on the figures surrounding my bed, peering down at me. My vision began to clear as blurred edges became crisp.

"Vail. Trevor. Otto," I choked out the words through a raw, burning throat.

The young fox jumped on top of me and licked my face. Otto flew up in the air and somersaulted into a wall. I needed to cry with joy, but I had no tears. My dry eyes could only blink back my feelings.

"You're home, baby! You're home!" Vail covered my mouth with his before showering kisses all over my face, competing with Trevor, Otto, and even Grump.

Mirror Mirror mumbled in the background.

"Home," I repeated, subconsciously letting out a deep breath I didn't need.

"Welcome to your death, sis." Ian patted my leg.

I stretched out my arms and took in my new senses. The clock beside me ticked loudly. A rat or squirrel or something scratched its way through the wall. Water dripped from a nearby faucet. And the smell of blood lingered in the air.

I jerked upright and bared my fangs, puncturing my bottom lip. "Ow." I brought my hand to my mouth and touched the wound with my fingertip. "How am I supposed to get used to these things?" I pulled my finger back and examined the glowing blood smeared across the tip. The gnash on my lip began to repair itself immediately.

A shocked silence fell on the room. Vail, Ian, and Drake stared back at me in confusion.

I touched my lip again, but the wound had vanished.

"Did she just heal herself?" Drake asked in a high-pitched tone. "That's not possible!"

"Ladies and gentlemen"—Finn cleared his throat, and his expression grew eerily wild—"I think we've just evolved."

I snapped my eyes to Vail's and wondered what kind of mess I'd created.

FROM THE DESK OF FRITZI COX

Dear Reader,

I regret to inform you that the end of this book is the honest truth, and our innocent princess has turned into a vicious vampire. I've not embellished any facts or created my own turn of events. But my accounts of her fate have been confirmed.

A few weeks after Penelope left, I visited Abe's shop. He mentioned that a press release from *Starlight Press* had appeared on his desk days before. I inquired about the news journal, but he only shook his head and handed me the article.

FRIENDS. REDEMPTION. ICICLES. TRANSFORMED. ZINFANDEL. IGNITED.

These words tell the story of a lost soul conquering her curse and gaining a new life where there was none to be had. Though immortal souls have no fears, the grief of loss spares no one. Do not seek out answers where only death awaits. When we believe we've reached our end, we learn it's only the beginning. The truth awaits one day in a golden vial of hope. You'll be the first to know.

A rush of blood drained from my face. I handed the article back to Abe and asked where I could get a copy. He let me keep it and informed me the *Starlight Press* had been out of business for decades. This was the only print.

I immediately returned home to consult with my husband. He read the title aloud and pointed out the bold first letters in each word. It was a code. Penelope had written the article specifically for me.

After spending countless hours deciphering the meaning, we both concluded that Penelope was alive—yet not. She'd transformed into a vampire, presumably to truly return home. Though I didn't understand how her blood would act as a cure or if it was even possible now that she was no longer human.

It wasn't long after that I discovered more mysterious clues from long ago. But my knowledge of this is too dangerous to print in this book. I've purposely left this news out for your safety, but you can read more through this secure link if you dare. As the *Starlight Press* article stated, *Do not seek out answers where only death awaits*. Information is a weapon or a weakness. Choose your path.

I'm sure you can guess which path I chose. After waiting for news, clues, and rumors from the other side, I finally decided to investigate Bostwick for any signs of progress. I kept my distance from the small town to shield my family. But curiosity got the best of me, and I decided to place an anonymous phone call. To my surprise, the woman who answered called herself the Lady of Bostwick. And even though her voice cut like stone, a hint of royalty whipped through her words.

"It's not safe," she whispered before hanging up.

As always, I will report my discoveries as I learn them—as

long as I determine the information is safe. You can follow my adventure and read more about Princess Penelope's—or the Lady of Bostwick's—happily ever after in *Royally Revamped.*

One-click Royally Revamped today!

Signup for my NEWSLETTER to find more information on my latest releases, and claim your exclusive, free ebook!
https://kataddams.com/free-book

Join my Facebook group, D.T.F. (Dirty. Tough. Females), for news, sneak-peeks, and more!

ALSO BY FRITZI COX

Dirty South Series

Faking Second Chances

Schooling Professor Playboy

Playing Backstage with the Rockstar

Stroking the Boss's ... Ego

Mayday (FREE for Newsletter Subscribers)

DTF (Dirty. Tough. Female.) Series

On the Rox

Cream-Pied

Whip it Out

Just the Tip

FU (FORKS UNIVERSITY FASHION ACADEMY) SERIES

Just Between Us

This Means War

BUCK OFF RANCH SERIES

Josie Thatcher, Cowboy Catcher

Emma Jean, Heartbreak Queen

PARANORMAL ROMANTIC COMEDY

Ghosted

**WRITING PARANORMAL ROMANTIC COMEDY AS
FRITZI COX**

Royally Drained

For a complete listing of Kat Addams books, visit

https://kataddams.com

ACKNOWLEDGMENTS

As always, thank you to the biggest inspiration and motivation in my life—my daughter. You'll always be my sunflower princess, even when your dark teenage magic emerges.

Thank you to my editor, Jovana; my cover designer, Najla; my graphics designer, Katherine; all of my readers; and my entire DTF crew. You are what keeps me moving forward. You and deadlines. I'd write more, but I have to get my ass started on the next book. Promise you won't kill me for these cliff-hangers!

Thank you to my amazing man, The D, who also keeps pushing me forward because he refuses to let me quit. *One, two, three. One, two, three, three.* I'm getting there. Thank you for coming along on this adventure and leading this dance when I'd rather pull a Penelope and hide in a bathtub with wine.

Speaking of …

And lastly, thank you to wine, for giving me dreams of Bostwick and, on occasion, the uninhibited imagination to create. Galileo once said, "Wine is sunlight, held together by water." I think Princess Penelope and I can both toast to that.

ABOUT THE AUTHOR

Fritzi Cox is a dark soul with a wicked sense of humor. She regularly bathes in the blood of her enemies while sipping champagne and hashtagging her vibes. She's fond of plotting mayhem, writing spellbinding twists, and tickling her readers with an over-the-top sense of humor. Rumor has it, her alter ego, Kat Addams, is her spirit animal. Or is it the other way around? Either way, expect Fritzi to keep you on your toes!